THE KING
WHO WAS
AND WILL BE

THE WORLD OF KING ARTHUR
AND HIS KNIGHTS

THE KING
WHO WAS
AND WILL BE

THE WORLD OF KING ARTHUR
AND HIS KNIGHTS

KEVIN CROSSLEY-HOLLAND

ILLUSTRATED BY
PETER MALONE

Orion
Children's Books

MASSANUTTEN REGIONAL LIBRARY
DISCARD
Harrisonburg, VA 22801

Acknowledgments are gratefully made to the following for brief quotations: "The Arming of Sir Topaz" from Nevill Coghill, *The Canterbury Tales*, Penguin Books, 1951; *Sir Gawain and the Green Knight* translated by Keith Harrison, Black Willow Press, 1992; *The Anglo-Saxon Chronicle* translated by Dorothy Whitelock, Eyre and Spottiswoode, 1961; *The Once and Future King*, by T. H. White, Collins, 1958; and "Six of Arthur's Warriors" from *The Quest for Olwen* by Gwyn Thomas and Kevin Crossley-Holland, Lutterworth, 1988. All the other quotations from medieval sources have been modernised or translated by Kevin Crossley-Holland.

First published in 1998
by Orion Children's Books
a division of The Orion Publishing Group
Orion House
5 Upper Saint Martin's Lane
London   WC2H 9EA

Text © Kevin Crossley-Holland 1998
Illustrations © Peter Malone 1998

Designed by Lovegrove Associates

The right of Kevin Crossley-Holland and Peter Malone to be identified as the author and illustrator respectively of this work has been asserted.

A catalogue record for this book is available from the British Library.
Printed in Italy
ISBN 1 85881 381 6

FOR LINDA

SYDD YN GWYBOD LLE MAE
ARTHUR YN CYSGU

CONTENTS

Map of Arthur's Britain 12

Knights, Knighthood and Chivalry 14

Medieval Romance 18

Geoffrey of Monmouth 19

Tintagel 21

Little Boys 22

The Sword in the Stone 23

The Crusades 24

Merlin 26

The Thirteen Treasures of Britain 28

Culhwch and Olwen 30

Six of Arthur's Warriors 31

Lady of the Lake 33

Excalibur 34

The Round Table 36

The Matchless Knights 38

Sir Gawain 40

Winchester 41

Cities, Courts and Castles 42

How to Be a Butler 44

Camelot and Castle Life 45

What's in a Name? 50

Sir Kay 51

Troubadours and Trobairitz 52

Gifts 54

Kiss Me! 55

Courtly Love 56

Marie de France 58

In the Midnight Garden 59

Elaine, the Fair Maid of Astolat 60

The Leading Ladies 62

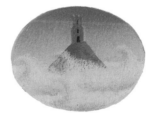

Dressing Your Lord 64

Food and Clothing 65

Verb that Carving! 70

The Wheel of Fortune 71

Guinevere   72

Sir Thomas Malory   74

Lancelot Goes Climbing   75

The Magicians   103

The Holy Grail   104

The Corpus Christi Carol   106

Sir Lancelot   76

Morgan le Fay   78

The Magical Objects   107

Arms and Armour   79

Sir Mordred   108

The Arming of Sir Topaz   82

Sir Bedivere   109

Tournaments and Tilting   84

Last Rites   110

Heraldry   88

Avalon and Glastonbury   112

Tristan and Isolde   90

Little Girls   92

Love   93

Medieval Art   94

Arthur's Britain   114

Wilderness   96

Companies of Beasts and Birds   116

Quests and Adventures   97

The King Who Was and Will Be   117

The Questing Beast   100

The First Book Printed in English 122

Magic and the Otherworld   101

Index   124

Arthur's Britain

This map is based on medieval sources that were sometimes imaginative, sometimes accurate.

🌿1 EDINBURGH where the extinct volcano is known as Arthur's Seat🌿 2 JOYOUS GARD Sir Lancelot's castle. Now called Alnwick or Bamburgh🌿 3 CARLISLE one of King Arthur's courts🌿 4 ANGLESEY where King Arthur sheltered in a cave between battles with the Irish🌿 5 RICHMOND where King Arthur and his knights may lie asleep🌿 6 BARDSEY where Merlin may still live in an invisible glass house🌿 7 DINAS EMRYS where a red dragon fought a white dragon in a subterranean lake🌿 8 SNOWDONIA where King Arthur fought the giant Ritho who made a cloak from the beards of men he had killed🌿 9 CHESTER one of King Arthur's courts🌿 10 THE GREEN CHAPEL where Sir Gawain journeyed to meet the Green Knight🌿 11 ALDERLEY EDGE where King Arthur and his knights may lie asleep🌿 12 CELIDON WOOD where King Arthur defeated the Saxons🌿 13 CARDIGAN one of King Arthur's courts🌿 14 CARMARTHEN where Merlin was born🌿 15 CRAG Y DINAS the Rock of the Fortress where King Arthur and his knights may be asleep🌿 16 CAERLEON King Arthur's Whitsun court🌿 17 MONMOUTH where Geoffrey, who wrote History of the Kings of Britain, was archdeacon🌿 18 DOZMARY POOL where Sir Bedivere threw Excalibur into the water🌿 19 TINTAGEL the birthplace of King Arthur🌿 20 CADBURY CASTLE an Iron Age hillfort sometimes believed to be Camelot🌿 21 GLASTONBURY where Joseph of Arimathea brought the Holy Grail, and where King Arthur and Queen Guinevere were buried🌿 22 MOUNT BADON where King Arthur defeated the Saxons. Now called Badbury Rings🌿 23 MARLBOROUGH where Merlin may lie buried in an earth mound🌿 24 CAMLANN where King Arthur fought his own son Mordred. Now called Salisbury Plain🌿 25 THE GIANTS' RING transported by Merlin from Ireland. Now called Stonehenge🌿 26 WINCHESTER one of King Arthur's courts. The home of the Round Table🌿 27 ASTOLAT where Elaine the White lived. Now called Guildford🌿 28 CANTERBURY whose archbishop was one of King Arthur's advisors🌿 29 DOVER where Sir Gawain's skull was kept in the castle🌿 30 COLCHESTER sometimes identified as Camelot🌿 31 CAMBRIDGE which received its charter from King Arthur🌿 32 YS the city that was submerged beneath the sea🌿 33 NANTES where Sir Erec was crowned King🌿 34 BROCELIANDE a magical forest. Now called the Forest of Paimpoint🌿 35 MONT ST MICHEL where King Arthur and Sir Bedivere slew a child-eating giant🌿

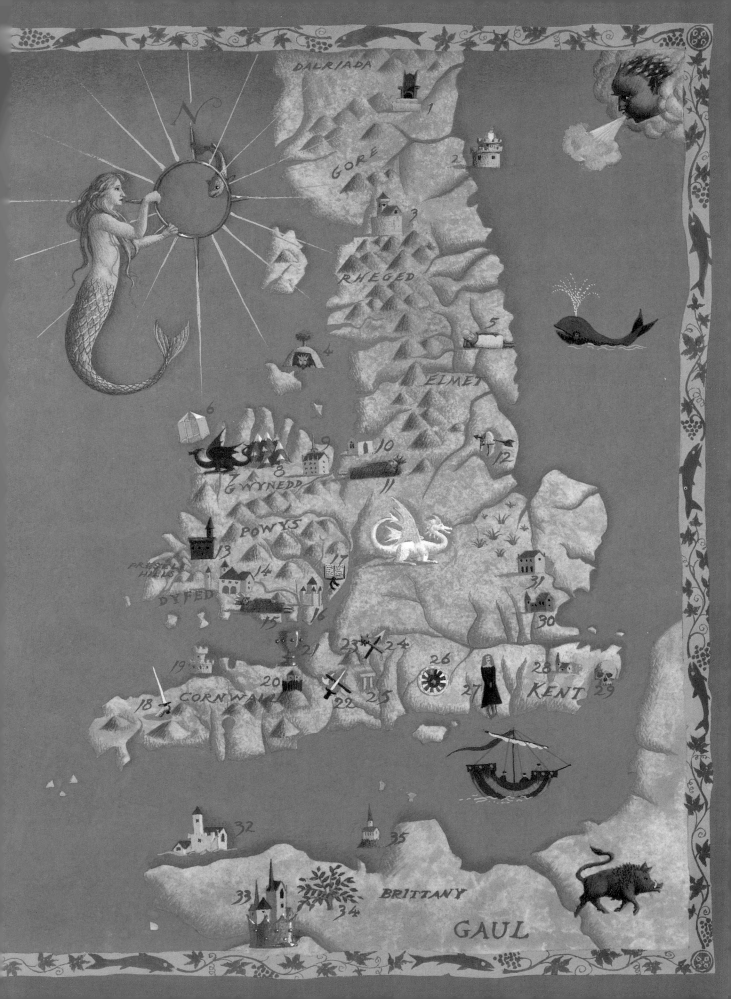

KNIGHTS, KNIGHTHOOD & CHIVALRY

The heroes of the Arthurian Romances are knights. Many of their enemies are knights as well. On almost every page there are knights vowing, knights praying, knights questing, knights fighting, knights rescuing, knights adoring. But who were they? In medieval Europe, who became a knight, and how? And what rules did a knight have to obey?

The word "knight" comes from the Anglo-Saxon *cniht*, meaning "household follower", and that is what the first knights were: men attached to the households of powerful lords, with duties to them that

14

included fighting. When men started to fight on horseback and wear elaborate armour, it became an expensive privilege to be a knight. So knighthood soon turned into an exclusive club for professional fighting men. To enter it, a young man needed not only to be well-born and well-off but to have trained and learned the rules. These rules are ideals most knights fell far short of, and the word we use to describe them is chivalry.

The first step on the road to knighthood was to become a page. A father and mother sent their son at the age of seven to live in the household of another knight, just as some parents today send their children to boarding schools. There, the young boy began to learn archery and swordsmanship, to hunt and hawk, and to learn good manners or courtesy. (The motto of Winchester College, a famous boys' school founded in the Middle Ages, is "Manners make the man".)

When you enter your lord's hall, say 'God Speed'
and greet everyone there cheerfully . . . Don't rush
in rudely, but walk in at an easy pace with your
head up, and kneel on one knee only to your lord.

After an apprenticeship of eight or nine years, the page became a squire, and sometimes still lived away from home. Now, he learned how to carve and serve at table; he trained with full-sized sword and lance; and he accompanied his father or lord to tournaments, or even abroad and into battle. But in *The Canterbury Tales*, the poet Geoffrey Chaucer shows how the squire did have time for more gentle pursuits, too:

> Singing he was, or fluting, all the day
> He was as fresh as is the month of May.
> Short was his gown, with sleeves long and wide.
> Well could he sit on horse, and fairly ride.
> He could make songs, and sing them well.
> Joust, and dance too, as well as draw and write.
> He was so hot a lover that at night
> He slept no more than does a nightingale.
> Courteous he was, humble, and quick to serve,
> And carved before his father at the table.

At the age of twenty or twenty-one, this chrysalis was at last ready to turn into a butterfly! Sometimes the ceremony of knighthood was simple, sometimes elaborate, with the squire keeping nightlong vigil in church, fasting, and putting on special clothing. Any knight could give another man knighthood by tapping his neck with a sword and pronouncing, "I dub you knight," and the ceremony could take place almost anywhere – on a battlefield, after a tournament, or in the peaceful great hall of a castle.

The code of chivalry required a knight to be Christian in word and deed, and ready to die for Christ just as Christ had died for him. A knight was expected to be patriotic, generous to friend and enemy, to protect people less well off than himself (especially widows, young women and orphans), and to right evil and injustice wherever he came across it.

Some writers thought the code of chivalry was a noble end in itself – a glorious ideal; some thought it was the way a knight could serve the lady he loved; and some (such as Chrétien de Troyes) argued that a dutiful knight always risked neglecting his lady while a dutiful lover always risked neglecting his knighthood.

What is clear is the gap between ideal and reality: in real life and in the romances, some knights were gentlemen, others were brutes. "Herein," writes William Caxton in his preface to the tales of knights by Sir Thomas Malory called *Le Morte d'Arthur*, "may be seen noble chivalry, courtesy, humanity, friendliness, hardiness, love, friendship, cowardice, murder, hate, virtue, and sin. Do after the good and leave the evil . . ."

MEDIEVAL ROMANCE

Between the twelfth and fifteenth centuries, writers all over Europe composed stories about ancient heroes. These stories, some in prose, some in verse, some combining the two, are known as romances, and they can be divided into three groups: the Matter of Rome (about classical heroes), the Matter of France (about Charlemagne and Roland), and the Matter of Britain (about King Arthur and his knights and lesser British figures).

The writers of romances were not in the least interested in what life was really like in ancient Rome or in the early Middle Ages. They cheerfully gave Arthur medieval attitudes and medieval clothing, and put him at the head of a court of knights and ladies caught up in quests and love matches and magical encounters.

Arthur was a hero throughout Europe and there are romances about him in eleven languages. The greatest were written by Chrétien de Troyes (French, late twelfth century), Gottfried von Strassburg (German, early thirteenth century), the unknown author of the magical and funny English

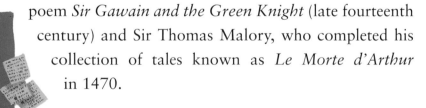

poem *Sir Gawain and the Green Knight* (late fourteenth century) and Sir Thomas Malory, who completed his collection of tales known as *Le Morte d'Arthur* in 1470.

GEOFFREY OF MONMOUTH

Who is first to tell us the amazing story of how Arthur was conceived? And who invented the wizard Merlin? Who first describes how Arthur, at the end of his life, crosses the water to Avalon? The answer to these questions is Geoffrey of Monmouth, a Welsh priest and teacher at the newly-founded university of Oxford, who was born around 1100 and died in 1154.

King Arthur is the central figure in the highly readable *History of the Kings of Britain*, which was a kind of best-selling, patriotic, historical novel written by Geoffrey to remind the Celts of their glorious past before they were overrun by the Anglo-Saxons, and to stir them up to win glory again. Geoffrey certainly drew on ancient tradition and it is possible that he made use (as he claims) of a "certain very ancient book in the British language" that no longer survives; but he also made a great deal up. You can think of this book as a kind of literary pearl: somewhere inside it there is a core of historical grit which is buried inside layers of shining invention.

Many medieval writers were attracted to Geoffrey's portrait of a warrior-hero-king in medieval clothing, and made use of it – just as William Shakespeare used Geoffrey's descriptions of Cymbeline and King Lear. Arthurian Romance is built on the foundations of *History of the Kings of Britain*.

TINTAGEL

According to Geoffrey of Monmouth in his *History of the Kings of Britain*, the castle at Tintagel is where the story of King Arthur really begins.

Uther Pendragon, King of Britain, falls in love with Ygerna, who is the wife of Gorlois, Duke of Cornwall. So great is his longing for her that he asks the magician Merlin to help him. Then Merlin gives Uther drugs which change his appearance so that he looks exactly like Gorlois.

Now Uther is able to walk straight past the castle guard in the twilight; he slips into Ygerna's arms in her bedroom, and all the time she supposes he is her own husband Gorlois. "And on that night, Arthur was conceived . . ."

Tintagel is on the rocky north coast of Cornwall. And as Geoffrey says, "The castle is built high above the sea, which surrounds it on all sides, and there is no other way in except that offered by a narrow isthmus of rock." The ruins now known as Arthur's Castle are in fact Norman, but remains of a stronghold close by date from the fifth or sixth century, the time of the "historical" Arthur. Visitors can also see rock formations known as Arthur's Chair, Arthur's Cup and Saucers, and Merlin's Cave.

Little Boys

Boys do not like work. They have big appetites and often get indigestion. Many little boys have bad habits. They shout and snatch greedily at whatever takes their fancy. They enjoy the talk and plans of boys like themselves and avoid the company of the old. They can't keep secrets but tactlessly repeat whatever they see or hear. They're quick to laugh, quick to cry, and keep up an endless noise and chatter morning, noon and night. As soon as they have been washed they make themselves absolutely filthy. They resist violently when their mothers wash them or

comb their hair. They think of nothing but their own stomachs, and are scarcely out of bed before they're clamouring for food.

ON THE PROPERTIES OF THINGS (A MEDIEVAL ENCYCLOPEDIA):
BARTHOLOMEW THE ENGLISHMAN

THE SWORD IN THE STONE

A massive square slab of stone appears in a London churchyard. Lying on the stone is a steel anvil, and sticking into this anvil is a sword. There is gold lettering on the stone:

WHOSO PULLETH OUT THIS SWORD
OF THIS STONE AND ANVIL IS RIGHTWISE KING
BORN OF ALL ENGLAND.

What a tremendous image and what a challenge! Who and where is the man or boy who can show he has God's approval as rightful king?

Sir Ector and his son Sir Kay come to London to joust on New Year's Day. When Kay leaves his sword behind, he asks his young foster-brother Arthur to go back for it. But Arthur finds the house locked, and rides straight to the churchyard. "And so," says Sir Thomas Malory, "he handled the sword by the handles, and lightly and fiercely pulled it out of the stone."

At this moment, not even Arthur realizes that he is indeed the rightful king, for his foster-father Sir Ector has closely guarded the secret of his birth and royal blood. When Arthur gives the sword to his elder brother, Kay at first deceitfully claims that he should be king; and then the barons object to being ruled by a fifteen-year-old boy. But Arthur repeats the feat, and at Easter the people of England cry: "We will have Arthur for our king, and delay no longer; for we all see it is God's will that he shall be our king."

THE CRUSADES

Women and men living in Europe in the Middle Ages did not doubt the existence of God. They knew God existed; they knew that everything that happened, good and bad, was part of God's plan, and knew that there was only one true faith – Christianity. People who worshipped in another faith were known as infidels.

At the end of the eleventh century, Pope Urban called Christians to arms to recapture Jerusalem, the birthplace of Christianity, which had been in infidel Muslim hands since 638 AD. This was the reason for the First Crusade in 1095 and the five Crusades and lesser efforts, spread over almost three centuries, that followed it. Crusades were military expeditions to win back sacred ground. "It is a clear sign," said Cardinal Odo, "that a man burns with love of God and zeal for God when he leaves country, possessions, house, children and wife, going overseas in the service of Jesus Christ."

Under the leadership of Richard the Lion Heart, Frederick Barbarossa, King Philip of France and Duke Godfrey of Bouillon, thousands of knights and common people from all over Europe enlisted in these Holy Wars, each stitching a red cross to his shoulder, each vowing not to turn back before he reached Jerusalem. But although Jerusalem was captured in 1099, it was only held for 88 years before it was retaken by the Turkish leader, Saladin.

For all their personal weaknesses, and the times when their enthusiasm boiled over into fanaticism and cruelty, the Crusaders shared the ideal of knighthood called chivalry: to show moral courage and physical courage, to care for the disadvantaged and weak, to be courteous to women, to right wrong, and to uphold the Christian faith. So it is true to say that the Crusades and many of the quests in Arthurian Romance, in particular the quest for the Holy Grail, have a great deal in common.

MERLIN

The magician Merlin casts a spell over readers of Arthurian romance. When he is onstage, we can scarcely take our eyes off him, and when he is offstage we wonder what he is up to. We may even catch ourselves thinking the whole story of Arthur is, somehow, Merlin's invention.

Merlin was born at Carmarthen ("Merlin's town") in Wales, the son of an evil spirit and a nun. As a boy, he persuades King Vortigern to dig up two fighting dragons, one red, one white, and explains the red one stands for the Celts, the white one for the Saxons. Merlin makes many prophecies but says that future events "cannot be revealed except where there is the most urgent need. If I were to utter them as an entertainment . . . the spirit which controls me would forsake me in the hour of need."

Merlin also helps Vortigern's successor by transporting the circle of massive bluestones at Stonehenge, weighing up to five tons each, from Ireland to England; and he helps King Uther by giving him magical drugs so that he can impersonate the Duke of Cornwall and make love to his wife, Ygerna, who conceives Arthur.

So Arthur is the fourth ruler who Merlin assists. He is, so to speak, Arthur's midwife, and spirits him away to his foster-parents, Sir Ector and his wife, wrapped in a gold cloth. Then he contrives the appearance in a London churchyard of the sword in the stone – the very proof of Arthur's kingship. He gives the young king effective military advice, and helps him to secure Excalibur from the Lady of the Lake; and he warns Arthur against marrying Guinevere. Merlin's role is to be Arthur's teacher, preparing him for kingship, guiding his first steps as king.

Some sources say Merlin became infatuated with his apprentice, Nimue, and that she shut him up in a rock; some say he was buried at

Carmarthen, or in the grounds of Marlborough ("Merlin's borough") College. But maybe he is still alive in an invisible glass house, perhaps on the island of Bardsey. Or did he go mad and run wild in the forest, until his sister Ganieda built him an observatory from which he still studies the stars?

Merlin may be a name, but it may be a description – a merlin or, in Welsh, a myrddin – of someone who has genius or divine inspiration. The Merlin of Arthurian romance is largely Geoffrey of Monmouth's brilliant invention, based on ancient British traditions and religious beliefs. Prophet and enchanter, trickster, shape-shifter and wise guide, Merlin is like an all-knowing and unblinking eye, still watching us.

The Thirteen Treasures of Britain

At sea, or over the sea, Merlin has with him in his house of glass:

Arthur's cloak, which makes him invisible;

a sword that bursts into flame if any man except its owner draws it from its scabbard;

a drinking horn that fills itself with whatever drink you desire;

a chariot which, if you sit in it, carries you wherever you want to go;

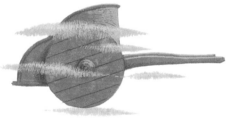

a whetstone which sharpens a brave man's sword but blunts the sword of a coward;

a platter that brings you whatever kind of food you would like to eat;

a red gown that hides whoever wears it;

a hamper that multiplies by one hundred times a helping of meat laid on it;

a knife with which to make sacrifices;

a cauldron which cooks only the food of a brave man;

a chess board made of gold, with silver chessmen who play themselves;

a mantle that keeps its wearer warm even in freezing weather;

a ring, so that you can see without being seen.

These treasures will remain in Merlin's safekeeping until the day when Arthur wakes, and returns, and is once again crowned king.

THE TRIADS (BRIEF SUMMARIES OF WELSH LEGENDARY BELIEFS):
ANONYMOUS

CULHWCH
&OLWEN

Long before Geoffrey of Monmouth inspired romance writers with his *History of the Kings of Britain*, Welsh poets and storytellers were already celebrating King Arthur. Few of their poems and stories have survived, but there is one masterpiece, the anonymous *Culhwch and Olwen* (late tenth century), which forms part of a cluster of eleven heroic tales known as *The Mabinogion*.

In this rollicking, fierce and magical tale, Arthur's followers include heroes familiar from medieval romance (Kay, Bedivere and Gawain), historical figures (the historian-monk Gildas and the poet Taliesin) and characters with amazing supernatural powers, such as Sugyn, who can swallow so much of the sea as to strand 300 ships. Together, they help Arthur's nephew Culhwch perform forty tasks named by the giant Ysbaddaden and so win the giant's beautiful daughter, Olwen. The Arthur of this fabulous story may be king but he doesn't preside over a court of chivalrous knights; rather, he leads a fearsome war-band with magical powers and so he stands somewhere between the historical Arthur and the Arthur of medieval romance.

Six of Arthur's Warriors

Sgilti Light-foot

When Sgilti Light-foot went out on an errand for his lord, he never walked along a road. If there were trees beside the road, he would walk along the tops of them, and on a mountain side he would walk along the tips of grass blades.

Hot-sole

The bright fire that flashed from Hot-sole's feet whenever they struck anything hard was as hot as molten iron drawn out of a forge; he cleared the way for Arthur and his army.

Lip

When Lip was unhappy, he used to drop his lower lip down to his navel and throw his upper lip over his head like a helmet.

Ear son of Listener

If Ear was buried seven metres deep in the earth, he could still hear a tiny ant fifty miles away emerging from its ant-hill in the morning.

Strike son of Striker

Strike could stand in the Great Forest in Cornwall and hit a wren in Cold Ridge in Ireland right through its two legs.

Gwion Cat's Eyes

Gwion could throw a spear and strip a film of skin from a midge's eye without hurting the eye itself.

THE MABINOGION (ELEVEN WELSH MYTHOLOGICAL AND LEGENDARY TALES): CULHWCH AND OLWEN: ANONYMOUS

LADY OF THE LAKE

There are many lake spirits and lake fairies in Welsh and Cornish legends and folk-tales, and the magical Lady of the Lake is either one of them or a priestess of the goddess of water.

Lady of the Lake is a position (rather like Bishop of the Isles or Secretary of State), and is occupied by several women in different Arthurian legends. One lives in a beautiful palace inside a rock, and walks on water, and gives Arthur his sword Excalibur; one is beheaded by Sir Balin, who has just won the sword from the king, when she demands it back from him; and one catches Excalibur when Sir Bedivere throws it into the lake at Camlann, and waves it three times and disappears; one, who is a mermaid, brings up Lancelot of the Lake until he is fifteen; and one, called Nimue or Viviane or Nineve, is apprentice to Merlin. The magician is utterly beguiled by her beauty, but she contemptuously rejects his advances and, using the magic she has learned from him, imprisons him inside a rock.

Powerful and attractive, mysterious, vulnerable and vengeful: like lake waters, the Lady of the Lake is all these things.

EXCALIBUR

Excalibur is not the same as the Sword in the Stone. While out riding with Merlin, young King Arthur sees in the middle of the lake "an arm clothed in white samite (heavy silk), holding a fair sword in her hand". The Lady of the Lake tells Arthur to row out and take the sword and scabbard from the outstretched hand; and Merlin warns the king the scabbard is worth ten of the sword, "for while you are wearing the scabbard, you will never shed a drop of blood, however badly wounded you may be".

In the Middle Ages, a sword was very highly prized both for its value and as a symbol of knighthood, and it was often given a name. The word Excalibur may come from the Latin *chalybs*, meaning "steel", or from Celtic words meaning "hard" and "lightning". But either way, we can hear swordstroke sounds (ekk-kksss-ka!) within it.

With Excalibur, Arthur wins fearsome fights. But then his vengeful sister, Morgan le Fay, steals the scabbard; and when Arthur is grievously wounded at the Battle of Camlann, and does shed blood, he orders Sir Bedivere to throw the sword back into the water: "and there came an arm and a hand above the water and met it, and caught it, and shook it three times and brandished it, and then the hand and the sword vanished into the water."

THE
ROUND TABLE

It is helpful to think of the Round Table in two ways: as an object, and as an idea or ideal.

The object was an enormous circular wooden table, perhaps with a hole in the middle, which may have been made by Merlin, and may have been given to King Arthur as part of Guinevere's wedding dowry. Each of Arthur's knights had his own seat at this table. Different writers say there were 24 or 50, 140, 150, 200 and 250 places while one twelfth-century writer, Layamon, claimed that the Round Table could seat 1600 people and was actually made by a Cornish carpenter!

There were a number of Round Tables that were in circulation in the Middle Ages and one of them, now legless, hangs in the Great Hall at Winchester Castle. As a way of linking the royal House of Tudor to the Golden Age of King Arthur, Henry the Eighth later had this table painted in Tudor green and gold, with a Tudor rose in the middle.

The idea or ideal of the Round Table is one of friendship and chivalry: a fellowship of knights who all swear to serve and be loyal to King Arthur, and all share a resolve to champion the right and to fight against the wrong. The Round Table is first mentioned by the Norman writer Wace in 1155:

> Arthur had this Round Table so made that when his fine knights sat at it to eat, their positions should be equal, and they should all be served at exactly the same time. So no man there could boast he was superior to anyone else.

Sir Thomas Malory, however, tells the story in a different way. Merlin went to King Leodegrance of Cameliard, and told him that Arthur wanted to marry his daughter, Guinevere.

"That is the best news I have ever heard," said Leodegrance. "I would give Arthur land if I thought it would please him, but he has no need of more land; so I will send him a gift that will please him much more. I will send him the Round Table which his father Uther Pendragon gave to me. When it is complete, one hundred and fifty knights sit at it. I have a hundred good knights myself, but lack fifty, for so many have been killed during my reign."

So Leodegrance delivered his daughter Guinevere to Merlin, and the Round Table with one hundred knights, and they rode and travelled eagerly, now by water, now by land, until they reached London.

"I have long loved this fair lady," said Arthur, "so nothing could be as dear to me as her coming. And these knights with the Round Table please me more than any riches."

Le Morte d'Arthur: Sir Thomas Malory

In making the Round Table circular, romance writers were also trying to establish it as a kind of successor to the table used by Christ and his disciples at the Last Supper. When the traitor Judas stood up and ran away, his seat was left empty. In the same way, one place at the Round Table is left empty. This is known as the Perilous Seat, and the only knight who can sit in it safely is the most perfect one – the one who succeeds in his quest for the Holy Grail.

So medieval writers were making a firm connection between Arthur and his knights and Christ and his disciples: a connection between chivalry and religion.

The Matchless Knights

Sir Accolon He is the lover of Morgan le Fay. He and King Arthur fight without recognizing each other, and the king kills him.

Sir Agravain He is the son of King Lot and Morgause, and the brother of Gawain, Gareth and Gaheris. He ambushes Sir Lancelot in Queen Guinevere's bedchamber. In making his escape, Lancelot kills him and twelve other knights.

Sir Balin He comes from Northumberland, and kills a Lady of the Lake. His use of the Lance of Longinus as a weapon makes the Waste Land barren and leads to the quest for the Holy Grail.

Sir Bors He is one of the three knights who achieve the quest for the Holy Grail. Unlike Sir Perceval and Sir Galahad, he returns to Camelot to describe his adventures. He is killed while on a Crusade in the Holy Land.

Sir Brian des Isles He attacks King Arthur's kingdom with Sir Kay. But after being defeated, he becomes the king's steward.

Sir Breunor le Noire He is nicknamed La Cote Mal Taillee, because his surcoat is the wrong size and shape, but he vows to wear it until he has avenged the murder of his father. He kills a lion that charges into Camelot and is about to maul Queen Guinevere. His quest is to help Maledisant who begins by ridiculing him and ends by marrying him.

Sir Constantine He is the son of Sir Cador of Cornwall, and King Arthur's cousin. Arthur names him as his successor as King of Britain after the Battle of Camlann. The two sons of Sir Mordred rebel against him and he kills them.

Sir Dagonet He is King Arthur's jester or fool, and the king knights him because he makes everyone laugh. He does not go questing but prefers to stay safe at court!

Sir Erec His love for his beautiful wife Enide leads him to neglect his duties as a knight. He responds to criticism by leaving court with Enide, and shows her his valour by undertaking fearsome adventures. He is crowned King of Nantes.

Sir Gaheris He is brother of Gawain, Gareth and Agravain. Arthur banishes him for killing his own mother whom he discovers making love to Sir Lamorak. While rescuing Queen Guinevere from burning, Sir Lancelot accidentally kills Gaheris and his brother Gareth.

Sir Gareth He is a brother of Gawain, Gaheris and Agravain, and is nicknamed Beaumains because of his beautiful white hands. He comes to court in disguise and works as a kitchen boy before helping Lynette rescue her sister from the Red Knight of the Red Lands. He is accidentally killed by Sir Lancelot.

Sir Lanval His love of a fairy woman arouses Queen Guinevere's jealousy, because the queen greatly admires him herself.

Sir Loholt He is the son of King Arthur and either Queen Guinevere or Lionors. He is murdered by Kay.

Sir Owen This historical character, said to be the son of Morgan le Fay, lived in Cumbria at the end of the sixth century. His commitment to knightly adventures jeopardises his marriage to Laudine. He is sometimes called the Knight of the Lion because he saves a lion that is being attacked by a serpent.

Sir Palamedes He is a Saracen and is at first a pagan. He is in love with Isolde but is twice defeated in combat by Sir Tristan. He then becomes a Christian and the Duke of Provence.

Sir Perceval He achieves his quest for the Holy Grail, learns the secret words spoken by Jesus to Joseph of Arimethea, and remains at the Grail castle where he becomes the Fisher King. He is childlike and sometimes called the Holy Fool.

Note: Between 24 and 1600 knights are said to have had seats at the Round Table.

SIR GAWAIN

In the Middle Ages, particularly strong ties linked a man and his sister's son. This was the relationship between King Arthur and Sir Gawain, who was the son of Arthur's sister, Morgause, and King Lot of Orkney.

Medieval romances stretched Gawain's character in opposite directions. In the wonderful English poem known as *Sir Gawain and the Green Knight*, Gawain is an absolute model of bravery and courtesy, and yet what makes him especially appealing is that he is not quite perfect. He allows himself to be tempted by the beautiful wife of his host. He is a human being! Some French writers, though, show Gawain in a very different light – cheating, disloyal, bitter and violent. But on these points, everyone agrees: Gawain was one of the most important of Arthur's knights. Like the sun, he grew stronger hour by hour until noon, and then weaker hour by hour after noon; he rode a horse called Gringolet; and his terrible feud with his dearest friend, Sir Lancelot, who accidentally killed Gawain's brothers Gareth and Gaheris while saving Queen Guinevere from burning, was a mortal blow to the fellowship of the Round Table.

In 1485, the printer William Caxton listed the evidence which proved (he said) the existence of King Arthur and his fellowship: the king's tomb at Glastonbury, the Round Table at Winchester, the king's red wax seal at Westminster, Sir Lancelot's sword (he doesn't say where!) – and in Dover Castle, Sir Gawain's skull.

WINCHESTER

Winchester is the site of an important Roman town known as Venta Belgarum, and the capital of the Anglo-Saxon kingdom of Wessex when Alfred the Great (the only British monarch to have been called Great) was king. The massive cathedral, and Winchester College, and the timbered buildings surrounding them, all point to the city's continuing wealth and significance in medieval times. So it is not surprising that some romance writers imagined King Arthur held court at Winchester, or that Sir Thomas Malory (with one eye on the Round Table in the castle) concluded that Winchester and Camelot were one and the same place.

Many people believed this. King Henry the Seventh wanted people to connect the royal House of Tudor to the earlier Golden Age, so he called his heir Arthur and arranged for him to be baptized in Winchester Cathedral. Poor Arthur died while still a boy but Henry the Eighth had the Round Table repainted in Tudor colours and added a cameo-portrait of himself.

One of the most exciting and most fitting literary discoveries of the twentieth century was made in the library of Winchester College: a fifteenth-century manuscript which is the oldest known version of *The Whole Book of King Arthur and of His Noble Knights of the Round Table* by Sir Thomas Malory.

Cities, Courts and Castles

Caerleon

This Roman city, sometimes called the City of the Legion, was where King Arthur held his Whitsun court. It is where he hears and rejects demands that he should swear allegiance to the Roman Emperor.

Cardigan

This is one of King Arthur's courts, and where the king hunts for the white stag. Whoever kills it must choose the woman at court he thinks the most beautiful, and kiss her.

Camelot

This castle is the principal court of King Arthur, and the place where his knights sit at the Round Table.

Carmarthen

This is the city where Merlin was born, and it takes its name from him.

Carlisle

One of King Arthur's courts.

Chester

One of King Arthur's courts.

Corbenic
The castle where the Holy Grail
and the Spear of Longinus are kept
in the safekeeping of the maimed
Fisher King.

Dover
The castle where Sir Gawain's skull was kept.

Joyous Gard
This is Sir Lancelot's castle, and is either Bamburgh or
Alnwick. Lancelot brings Guinevere here after rescuing her
from the stake.

Tintagel
The castle of Gorlois, Duke of Cornwall, where Arthur was
conceived and born.

Winchester
A court of King Arthur. Winchester and Camelot may be one
and the same.

Hautdesert
The castle of Sir Bertilak, the Green Knight, who takes part in
a beheading contest with Sir Gawain.

How to be a Butler

Do not claw your head or back as if you were after a flea, and do not flatten your hair as if you were searching for a louse.

Don't be glum or gloomy, but don't twinkle; your eyes should neither wink nor water.

Don't pick your nose or let it drop clear pearls; and avoid sniffing or blowing your nose too hard, in case your master hears you.

Don't twist your neck like a jackdaw; don't wring your hands as if you were sawing wood; and don't puff up your chest, or pick your ears, or be slow of hearing.

Do not retch, or spit too far, or laugh or talk too loudly. Don't make faces or mimic others; and do not tell lies. You should not lick your lips or dribble.

Don't squirt saliva or juice out of your mouth, or gape or yawn, or pout. And don't try to clean a dusty dish with your tongue.

Good lad, don't pick or grind or gnash your teeth; and never huff and puff bad breath up your master's nose.

BOOK OF NURTURE (A MANUAL DESCRIBING HOW TO BEHAVE IN POLITE SOCIETY): JOHN RUSSELL

44

CAMELOT & CASTLE LIFE

It's no good wondering where Camelot was. It was never a place on a map. Camelot existed only in human heads and human hearts – as it still does.

True, there was a shadowy sixth-century Celtic leader who stopped the Saxons in their tracks, a man whom we call "Arthur"; and true again, this "Arthur" would have lived in an Iron Age hillfort such as Cadbury Castle in Somerset. The sixteenth-century writer John Leland went one tantalizing step further: "At the very south end of the church of South-Cadbyri standeth Camallate, sometime a famous town or castle . . . The people can tell nothing there but that they have heard say that Arthur much resorted to Camelot." But that is as far as we can go.

Perhaps a better question than "Where was Camelot?" is "What was Camelot?" In the same way that British monarchs now divide their time between London and Windsor, Sandringham and Balmoral, King Arthur regularly moved from one residence to another: Carlisle, Winchester, Cardigan, Caerleon . . . The castle Camelot was the king's principal residence. But it was also the name of the town surrounding his castle. Camelot was where knights took their places at the Round Table - the very symbol of fellowship and chivalry. And since it was where King Arthur held court, it was also the home of justice. The Holy Grail appeared fleetingly at Camelot, and it was the point of departure for knights questing for the Holy Grail.

The miserable entry for 1137 AD in the *Anglo-Saxon Chronicle* reads:

> For every powerful man built his castles . . . and they filled the country full of castles. When the castles were built, they filled them with devils and wicked men. Then, both by night and

day, they took those people that they thought had any goods, and . . . tortured them with indescribable tortures to extort gold and silver. They were hung by the thumbs or by the head, and heavy armour was hung on their feet. Knotted ropes were put round their heads and twisted until they penetrated to the brains. They put them in prisons where there were adders and snakes and toads, and killed them like that.

These vivid words describe exactly what eleventh- and early twelfth-century Norman castles were for: they were fortresses and prisons designed to protect and increase the power of their owners. At the same time they were the draughty, stony homes of the country's leading families and their households. Safety came first, comfort a poor second.

But during the next three hundred years, safety and comfort slowly exchanged places, and this is reflected in the descriptions of Camelot and other residences in the romances. First kings forbade their noblemen to build heavily-fortified castles; then warfare went abroad – to France, to Jerusalem – and with England itself reasonably peaceful, there was no longer any need to build defences such as motte and bailey and keep. Decoration began to be as important as defence:

> . . . Clusters of painted pinnacles, cleverly joined,
> Their high carved tops, far up in the sky.
> He also caught sight of the chalk-white chimneys
> That shimmered immaculately on the tower-tops:
> From any vantage-point so many turrets and towers
> Amid the parapets! – and scattered so thickly
> It seemed a pure fancy, or a model made out of paper.

Finally, knights stopped fortifying their homes altogether. They built two- (or occasionally three-) storey manor houses, sometimes of timber and plaster, sometimes of stone. Even the kitchen and pantry and bedrooms and other small rooms had glass windows, while the heart of the house was still the great hall, by day a kind of office from which the lord ran his estate farms and attended to other business, and in the evening a dining-sitting-room where the family ate, drank, entertained guests, sometimes sang, sometimes sewed, wrote letters, learned French, and played dice and draughts and chess.

A house like this often had an entrance on the upper floor, reached by a steep flight of steps; and sometimes it was surrounded by a moat which also usefully served as a fishpond. But these were no more than sensible precautions. Each family's own Camelot may have needed Keep Out signs and watchdogs, but people living in a late medieval manor did not feel themselves to be any more or less at risk than a family living in a large country house today.

WHAT'S IN A NAME?

In recent years, it has become quite commonplace for parents to name their baby before it has even been born. But there is nothing new about this. In the Middle Ages, one family sometimes used only a handful of names throughout many generations, and it's not uncommon to find that the eldest son or daughter in one family was called by the same name – John, say, or Joan, Henry or Mary – for many generations; or that when a baby or young child died, its younger sibling would then be given the same name.

When they grew up, people were often given second names, almost nicknames, that described one of their key characteristics. Here are some of the second names of King Arthur's warriors listed in the Welsh *Mabinogion*: Flamelord, Rich-in-Cattle, Steel-King the Hunchback, Hundred Claws, Reed-Cutter, Iron Fist, Son of Seventh, Mighty Thigh, Little Son of Three Cries, Enough, Watch-Dog, Red, Striker, Someone, Dry-Lip, Cutbeard, Angel-Face, Light-Foot, Old Right, Scorn, Red-Eye the Stallion, Generous, Old Face, Restless.

SIR KAY

How difficult to kneel in front of your younger brother and swear to obey him! Kay tries to claim the kingship for himself when his younger brother Arthur hands him the sword he has drawn from the stone; but when Arthur pulls it out again in front of their father, Sir Ector, Kay is forced to bend his knee. Arthur then generously asks him to be manager of the royal household.

How uncomfortable, too, to have to be the elder brother of a king! Is this one reason why Kay is sometimes surly or angry, and sometimes deliberately stirs up trouble? He mocks other people, and they laugh at him: he is often the salt-and-pepper in the Camelot stew, while one legend says he actually murdered Loholt, Arthur's own son, and rebelled against the king.

But there is another side to Cai, as the Welsh called him. Their Arthurian stories, which are the oldest, show him as virile and hard-drinking, an implacable warrior with a body as hot as a furnace, able to hold his breath underwater for nine days and do without sleep for nine nights, and make himself tall as a tree. Values in medieval European society were much more genteel than those of the fierce Celtic tribal world where stories were first told about Kay; so this, too, explains why the later English, French and German writers loved to disapprove of him.

TROUBADOURS
& TROBAIRITZ

Troubadours were minstrel-poets living in Provence in the south of France during the twelfth and early thirteenth centuries. Their subject was love:

> Noble lady, I ask nothing of you but that you should accept
> me as your servant. I will serve you as a good lord should be
> served, whatever the reward may be. Here I am, then, at
> your orders, sincere and humble, gay and courteous.
> You are not, after all, a bear or a lion, and you will not
> kill me, surely, if I put myself between your hands.

In troubadour poems, the lover adores a woman who is higher-born than he is, and another man's wife. He praises her beauty. He is ready to serve her in any way she wishes. If she returns his love, he rejoices; if she rejects him, he suffers but doesn't stop loving her. For his love enriches him:

> Each day I am a better man and purer for I serve the noblest
> lady in the world, and I worship her, I tell you this in the open.

These attitudes are sometimes called courtly love, and writers of Arthurian Romance made much use of them.

Troubadours composed and sang their poems of love-longing (with lute accompaniment) to entertain noblemen and noblewomen in the courts of Provence. And trobairitz (women poets), meanwhile, sang their own fresh and realistic love songs, in which men are no longer humble worshippers and women speak from the heart:

Friend, if you had shown consideration, meekness, candour and humanity, I'd have loved you without hesitation, but you were mean and sly and villainous.

We don't know whether courtly love was a poetic fantasy idealizing women – a sort of literary safety-valve – or what really happened among a tiny percentage of the population, the knights and ladies attached to medieval royal households in France. It is difficult to believe there could be so much smoke without some fire! But in any case the troubadours (and after them the trouvères in northern France and the minnesingers in Germany) were breaking completely new ground, for their love songs were composed at a time when young women were entering marriages arranged for political or economic reasons, and obeyed their husbands, and had few rights.

Today, we take the idea of romantic love for granted. We say that we "fall in love". For centuries, books and songs have shown love between men and women as the most wonderful experience in life, and we would like to believe that no obstacle in the world can stop true love from having its way. The first people to sing and say such things were the troubadours.

GIFTS

In real life and in Arthurian Romance, courtly love was like an elaborate game or even like an imaginary country. The women and men who played it, or lived in it, were expected to stick to all kinds of laws and rules. One of these concerned the receiving of presents, and this is what the monk who wrote the rulebook has to say: "A woman who loves a man may accept the following gifts from her lover without a guilty conscience: a handkerchief, a fillet for her hair, a wreath with gold or silver leaves, a breastpin, a mirror, a belt, a purse, a tassel, a comb, sleeves, gloves, a ring, a powder compact, a cameo, a wash basin, little dishes, trays, a toy flag as a memento and . . . any small present which helps her with her own appearance or is pleasing to look at or reminds her of her lover, provided it is quite clear (to her lover) she did not expect such a gift or have any right to it."

Kiss Me!

"Kiss me! Kiss sweet!" That's what your lips repeat.

Oh! yes. That's always how it seems to me.

But Caution stands so close it cannot be,

and that's the reason for my aching heart.

But keep your word now herc alone we meet,

Give me a sweet sweet kiss or two or three!

"Kiss me! Kiss sweet!" That's what your lips repeat.

Oh! Yes. That's always how it seems to me.

Caution hates me – just why, I can't make out –

And wrecks my dreams and tries to ruin me.

God grant that I may see him burn and die,

And live to stamp his ashes underfoot!

"Kiss me! Kiss sweet!" That's what your lips repeat.

Oh! yes. That's always how it seems to me.

Song: Charles D'Orleans
(early fifteenth-century French poet)

55

COURTLY LOVE

Late in the twelfth century, a French monk known as Andreas Cappellanus wrote a kind of handbook for lovers. Courtly love, he says, consists of the passionate and illicit adoration of a man for a married woman (not his wife); he must praise her beauty and character, be obedient to all her wishes and be willing to serve his lady and undergo torment:

> Love is suffering; that is easy to see. Until a man and woman love one another equally, there is no greater torment, since the lover keeps trembling for fear he will not win the loved one, and is wasting his efforts . . . And if he is a poor man, he worries the woman may turn up her nose at his poverty; and if he's ugly, he's afraid she will judge him by his looks and bestow her affections on a more handsome man; and if he's rich, he's troubled that his meanness in past times may catch up with him. To tell the truth, no one can count all the different fears within one lover's heart.

Many writers of Arthurian Romance were attracted to the ideals of courtly love; and in his *Lancelot*, Chrétien de Troyes shows how a knight must never flinch or hesitate in the service of his lady, even if it means he has to behave in a way unfitting or dishonourable for a knight. In one scene, Guinevere loses her temper with Sir Lancelot because he is more concerned with losing face than with her wishes, and hesitates before riding to see her by the first means available – a cart normally used for transporting murderers and thieves. So what Chrétien is saying is that it was even more important and more difficult to be a perfect lover than to be perfectly chivalrous.

The relationship of Lancelot and Guinevere and Tristan and Isolde both include elements of courtly love such as service, the great passion of "noble hearts", and suffering; but, like all the world's greatest love stories, each rewrites the rules of love and deepens our understanding of it.

MARIE DE FRANCE

"And now, at the end of this text, which I have written in French, I will name myself so that people may remember me: my name is Marie and I come from France." But who was she – Marie de France?

We only know for sure that she was well-born and well-educated, lived during the late twelfth century either in France or England, and is the earliest known French woman poet.

What interested Marie was love, and the way lovers behave, and she wrote delicious short story-poems known as lays, full of love's joy, anxiety and suffering, two of which have Arthurian subjects. One (*Chevrefoil*) is about the intense love of Tristan and Isolde, and another concerns Lanval, a knight of the Round Table, who falls in love with a beautiful fairy woman. She promises that whenever Lanval summons her, she will come to his side unseen and do whatever he asks – but on one condition: "not to reveal this secret to anyone . . . you would lose me forever if this love were to become known." But this is a fairytale, and after a trial set at King Arthur's court it has a happy ending!

In the Midnight Garden

And she got up and put on her fine silk gown; then she collected her bedclothes and towels, and tied them end to end, and made a rope as long as she could, and fastened it to a window-bar; and so she let herself down into the garden.

Then she gathered her dress with one hand in front of her and one hand behind her, and lifted it, because she saw the dew lay heavy on the grass, and made her way down the garden . . .

Her little breasts swelled beneath her clothes like two walnuts. And her waist was so slender that your two hands could have encircled her; and the daisies snapped beside her toes and, lying on the bridge of her foot, they looked all black beside her feet and ankles, so perfectly white was the girl's skin.

AUCASSIN AND NICOLETTE
(A FRENCH ROMANCE): ANONYMOUS

ELAINE, THE FAIR MAID OF ASTOLAT

Elaine falls wildly in love with Sir Lancelot, and persuades him to tie her scarlet sleeve embroidered with pearls to his helmet, as a sign of her love. In doing this, Lancelot is devious (he wants the sleeve to help disguise his identity while jousting) and rather unwise. For he does not return Elaine's love, and declines to marry her or take her as a lover.

"Alas! Then," said she, "I must die for your love."

For ten days Elaine neither eats nor sleeps nor drinks; then she asks her brother to write out a letter. When she dies, this letter is put into Elaine's right hand, and her richly-dressed corpse is laid in a barge covered with black silk, and steered down the River Thames to Westminster. King Arthur himself opens Elaine's letter: "Most noble knight, my lord Sir Lancelot, now death has divided us because of my love for you. For I loved you, and men called me the Fair Maid of Astolat. To all the women in the world I raise my cry . . ."

So Elaine the White, as Sir Thomas Malory calls her, is the very embodiment of unrequited love. Lancelot praises her character and beauty but says, "I much dislike being forced to love, for love can only spring from the heart itself, and not from force."

The Leading Ladies

Elaine of Astolat Sometimes called Elaine the White, she is a young woman who falls in love with Sir Lancelot. When he does not return her love, she fasts and dies, and her body is carried on a barge down the River Thames to Westminster.

Enide She is the beautiful, loyal and forbearing wife of Sir Erec who fearlessly accompanies her husband on his knightly adventures.

Ettard She does not return Sir Pelleas' love for her. Nimue casts two spells as a result of which she falls in love with Pelleas and he no longer loves her. She dies of a broken heart.

Guinevere She is the beautiful and passionate daughter of King Leodegrance of Cameliard. As the wife of King Arthur, she is the leading lady at Camelot. She has a long and stormy affair with Sir Lancelot, and ends her days as a nun.

Isolde She is the daughter of King Anguish of Ireland, and marries King Mark of Cornwall. But the man she loves is Sir Tristan, the king's nephew, and they have a wild and tragic love affair.

Laudine of Landuc She is married first to Esclados, who guards the magic fountain in the forest of Broceliande, and second to Sir Owain, after he has killed her first husband.

Lionors She is a lover of King Arthur, and may be the mother of his son, Sir Loholt.

Lunette She is a charming fixer. After learning magic from her cousin Nimue, she creates a magic fountain in the forest of Broceliande in Brittany, and sometimes wears a ring that makes her invisible. She helps Sir Owain to win her mistress, Laudine.

Lynette She comes to Arthur's court to ask for help for her sister Lyonesse, whose land is being attacked by the Red Knight of the Red Lands. The kitchen boy Beaumains is her champion and, not realising he is Gareth in disguise, she is scornful and caustic until he proves himself in combat.

Lyonesse She rules the lost land of Lyonesse, and the Red Knight of the Red Lands is trying to win it from her. Sir Gareth rescues her and her realm, and she marries him.

Maledisant She is a young woman helped by Sir Breunor. At first she taunts him because his clothes are so badly cut, but in the end she marries him.

Morgause She is King Arthur's sister, and their incestuous son is Sir Mordred. She marries King Lot of Orkney, and their sons are Gawain, Gareth, Gaheris and Agravain. Gaheris kills her when he finds her making love to Sir Lamorak.

Moronoe She is the sister of Morgan le Fay.

Olwen She is the daughter of the giant Ysbaddaden. She wants to marry Culhwch but he has to perform astonishing tasks, helped by King Arthur and his followers, before they become man and wife.

Ygerna She is the mother of King Arthur. Her first husband is Gorlois, Duke of Cornwall, and her second is Arthur's father, Uther Pendragon.

Dressing Your Lord

Humbly ask your lord to come and stand or sit beside the fire, where it is warm, and get dressed there; and wait politely to assist him. First hold out his tunic for him, and then his doublet while he puts in his arms, and have his waistcoat well-aired so that it is not damp, likewise his ankle socks, and then he will stay warm all day.

Pull up his socks and his leggings at the fireside, and lace or buckle his shoes, draw up his breeches and tie them at the height that suits him, lace every hole of his doublet, and put a kerchief round his neck and across his shoulders; and then gently comb his hair with an ivory comb, and give him water with which to wash his hands and face.

Then get down on one knee and say: "Sir, what cloak or gown would you like to wear today?" Fetch him the one he asks for, and hold it out for him to put on; then secure his belt, tightly or loosely, arrange his gown so that it hangs right, give him a hood or hat for his head, a cloak or a cape, depending on whether the weather is fair or foul, or all misty with rain; and in this way you will please him.

Before he leaves, brush him down thoroughly, and whether he is wearing satin, silk, velvet, scarlet or crimson cloth, make sure everything is completely clean and very smart.

BOOK OF NURTURE: JOHN RUSSELL

FOOD AND CLOTHING

In the industrialized world, there is an ugly gap between the living standards of the rich and the poor. In the Middle Ages, however, the gap was even greater and few people tried to do anything to narrow it. The Arthurian Romances revolve around court and castle life, and paint a picture of people who ate lavishly and dressed sumptuously, and quite literally wore their wealth on their sleeves. Chrétien de Troyes describes how Queen Guinevere gives penniless Enide a tunic and mantle, and says: "even the sleeves of this tunic were lined with white ermine. There were more than two hundred marks (1 mark: 8 ounces) of beaten gold, at the wrist and neck, and everywhere large jewels – violet, green, deep blue, grey-brown – were let into the gold."

A family (usually an extended family) and its servants, living in their castle or manor house, were largely self-sufficient. The wife was a sort of glorified farmer's wife, in charge of bakehouse and smokehouse, dairy and brewery, keeping hens and pigs, preserving fruit, drying and salting meat and fish, as well as actually providing substantial meals at ten o'clock and four o'clock each day. But she had to buy in salt, spices and sweeteners such as dates, sugar loaves and treacle; oranges and lemons; seafish; and wine from France, Gascony and Germany.

In many romance feasting scenes, the host seems to take a delight in showing off his wealth by providing expensive delicacies (such as baked sturgeon, roast swan, boar's head) and providing far more food than his guests could possibly eat:

Serving-men, with becoming grace, brought bowls
Of several excellent soups, exquisitely seasoned,
Brimming over and steaming – then dishes of various fish:
Some baked in bread, some broiled on the embers,
Some boiled, or stewed with spices in their juice –
All served with delicate sauces . . .

Sir Bercilak apologizes to Sir Gawain for this meal and promises they will eat better the next day!

The woman at the head of a great house not only supervised food supplies but was also responsible for clothing – spinning, weaving and dyeing, cutting out and making garments and household linen. She had to be practical and hard-headed, but there is also plenty of evidence that she (and her husband) were quality- and fashion-conscious. In 1440, Agnes Paston wrote from Norfolk to her husband William: "The gown needs to be bought, and the colour ought to be a good blue or else a bright blood-red. Please buy me two reels of gold thread. Your fish ponds are doing well."

Women and men both wore shifts which were undergarments of soft and sometimes fine material with long sleeves. Over this, the ladies of the romances wore magnificent dresses with laced bodices and long skirts, often embroidered or trimmed with fur or decorated with stones. A knight's tunic was also long-sleeved but only came down to his knees. Tunics were fastened with a brooch or clasp, as was the sleeveless cloak worn by both sexes when it was wet or cold.

Arthurian Romances, medieval chronicles, manuals and letters regularly delight in describing clothing and jewellery: "shifts made of Indian silk . . . mantles of green velvet trimmed with grey fur . . . shoes snouted and picked more than a finger long, crooking upwards, resembling devil's claws, and fastened to knees with chains of gold and silver." Such descriptions not only display the most lively pleasure in colour, shape and changing fashion but are intended to show off the wealth and good taste of their owners. The very appearance of knight and lady is a statement of their social position.

Chrétien de Troyes ends his romance of *Erec and Enide* with a coronation scene. Before Sir Erec is crowned King of Nantes, King Arthur dubs four hundred new knights and gives them clothing to fit their new status: "he did not give mantles made of serge, not of rabbit or dark-brown wool, but of samite (heavy silk) and ermine, of whole miniver (an imaginary animal covered in white fur) and mottled silk, bordered with orphrey (gold thread embroidery), stiff and rough." Most fittingly, Erec's own coronation robe, made by four fairies, portrays four ladies representing the cornerstones of medieval wisdom: Geometry and Arithmetic, Music and Astronomy. And this robe's fur lining "was from strange beasts that have completely blond heads and necks as black as mulberries and backs that are bright red on top, with black bellies and indigo tails. Such beasts are born in India, and are called *berbiolettes*."

Verb that Carving!

Here are some of the terms to be used when one is carving:

Break that deer – sauce that capon – spoil that hen –

unbrace that duck – unlace that rabbit – dismember that heron –

display that crane – disfigure that peacock –

unjoint that bittern – wing that partridge –

mine that plover – thigh that pigeon – chin that salmon –

string that lamprey – side that haddock –

tame that crab – splat that pike.

BOOK OF KERVING: WYNKYN DE WORDE
(AN EARLY SIXTEENTH-CENTURY PRINTER APPRENTICED TO WILLIAM CAXTON)

THE WHEEL OF FORTUNE

"What goes up must come down": that is the idea behind the turning Wheel of Fortune. To illustrate how humans are only human, with fortunes that rise and fall, medieval writers and painters showed the classical goddess Fortuna holding a great wheel, with nine heroes (or Worthies) clinging to the inside of the rim, some on the way up, some on the way down.

Three of these Nine Worthies were Biblical (Joshua, David and Judas Maccabaeus), three were pagans (Hector, Alexander the Great and Julius Caesar) and three were Christian knights (Charlemagne, King Arthur, and Duke Godfrey of Bouillon who led one of the Crusades).

King Arthur has a dream in which he sees Fortuna and her wheel. At first, the goddess favours him:

> You will sit in the high chair, I choose you myself
>
> Above all the leaders acclaimed on earth . . .
>
> Rest, royal king, for Rome is your own!

But without reason Fortuna's mood suddenly worsens. She warns Arthur he has "enjoyed comforts and kingdoms enough":

> Then she whirls the wheel and whirls me off and under
>
> So my four quarters were crushed and broken into pieces!
>
> And my spine was chopped in two by that chair!

When Arthur tells one of his advisers about this nightmare, he is in no doubt what the king must do:

> Man, mend your ways before you meet with disaster
>
> And humbly beg mercy for the saving of your soul!

GUINEVERE

Most of the ladies floating round Camelot are rather beautiful, faceless playthings. But Guinevere is not in the least like this. Wife of King Arthur, queen of Camelot and lover of Sir Lancelot, she is a powerful and passionate woman.

This may be because Guinevere existed long before Arthurian Romance. She is a shadowy figure from early British history, like King Lear or King Cole or King Arthur himself. She has the same authority as tribal leaders such as Boudicca who ruled their own territory, chose their own husbands and lovers, and led their own armies. Medieval writers would have admired Guinevere's spirit but disapproved of her independence, and this may be why they portray her in such a contradictory way: generous yet jealous, dutiful yet wilful, noble yet faithless.

The passionate affair of Guinevere and Lancelot is one of the great love stories of the western world, comparable to Tristan and Isolde (another Arthurian story) and Romeo and Juliet. Lancelot is Arthur's foremost knight and trusted friend. But he falls in love with Guinevere, and this love spurs him to deeds which bring ever greater glory to Camelot. When troublemakers reveal their relationship to the king, Guinevere is sentenced to death by burning. At the last moment, Lancelot gallops to the rescue, but although he saves Guinevere, the Fellowship of the Round Table is doomed. Arthur pursues Lancelot to France, Mordred seizes the throne and forces himself on Guinevere, and the Golden Age of Camelot comes to an end.

What is so fascinating is that, although Guinevere is unfaithful to Arthur, she is never disloyal to him. She presides over Camelot alongside him and fulfils all her public duties as his queen. She never speaks one word against him, or thinks of breaking up her marriage to the man she respects but does not love.

In *Le Morte d'Arthur*, Sir Thomas Malory calls Guinevere a "true lover" and "most noblest Christian queen" and implies that what people do in private is their own business; those responsible for wrecking Camelot are not Guinevere and Lancelot but the troublemakers who insist on making private matters public.

But this is not quite what Malory has Guinevere herself believe. "Lancelot and I have caused all this strife," she says, "and the death of the most noble knights in the world; because of our love, my most noble lord lies slain."

After Arthur's death, Guinevere becomes a nun at Amesbury, and refuses to see Lancelot again. Some sources say she was buried with Arthur at Glastonbury. In 1191, monks found a grave with the king's name on it containing the bones of a man and a woman, and a lock of beautiful golden hair that crumbled to dust as soon as it was touched.

SIR THOMAS MALORY

The character of Sir Thomas Malory (c.1416-1471) is a fascinating puzzle. On the one hand, he went to prison eight times for rape, theft, cattle-rustling and blackmail, and maybe also for political crimes. On the other, he spent most of his prison years writing eight long tales about King Arthur and his knights that shine with generosity, honesty, loyalty, courtesy, bravery, and a very clear sense of right and wrong.

It is true Malory was not a deep thinker, and was more stirred by action in the field than by the subtleties of courtly love or mysteries of the Holy Grail; but he was a terrific storyteller with access to a wide range of sources, and all in all his tales are much the finest as well as the complete retellings of the Arthurian legends in English. They were published in 1485 under the title *Le Morte d'Arthur* by William Caxton, the man who brought the technique of printing to England.

Malory's work has been a source of inspiration for many later poets, novelists, painters and book illustrators, and makers of musicals and films.

Lancelot Goes Climbing

Then Sir Lancelot took his sword in his hand and stole to the place where he had spied a ladder earlier, and he gripped the ladder under his arm, and carried it through the garden and placed it beneath the window. And soon the queen was there ready to meet him . . .

"I wish," said the queen, "I wish as much as you that you could come up to me."

"Do you wish, madam," said Sir Lancelot, "with your heart that I were with you?"

"Yes, truly," said the queen.

"Then I shall prove my might," said Sir Lancelot, "because of your love."

First he climbed the ladder, and then he laid his hands on the bars of iron beneath the queen's window, and he pulled at them with such force that he ripped them right out of the stone walls, and one of the iron bars cut through the flesh of Lancelot's hands to the bone. And then he leaped into the bedroom to the queen.

Le Morte d'Arthur: Sir Thomas Malory

SIR LANCELOT

The "best knight in the world" is Lancelot of the Lake. He is King Arthur's most trusted companion, achieves unrivalled feats, becomes Queen Guinevere's lover, and embodies the ideal of chivalry:

> Ah! Lancelot. You were the finest of all Christian knights . . . none on earth could match your strength . . . You were the most loyal friend to your love who ever sat on a horse . . . and you were the kindest man who ever struck with sword. And you were the most courteous man who ever walked among a throng of knights, and you were the most meek and gentle who ever feasted with ladies in the hall, and you were the sternest knight to your mortal foe who ever couched spear in the rest.

So says Lancelot's greatest champion, Sir Thomas Malory.

Lancelot, son of King Ban, is reared by the Lady of the Lake. His castle is Joyous Gard (either Bamburgh or Alnwick). As a fighting man, he is unbeatable both in set-piece tournaments and during his adventures, when he performs literally hundreds of astonishing deeds such as smashing his way through a throng of knights to rescue Queen Guinevere from burning at the stake, crossing into the land of Gorre on a terrifying bridge made entirely of swords, and plucking a lady from a bathtub full of boiling water. But he cannot quite achieve the greatest quest, for the Holy Grail, because of his sinful affair with Guinevere.

Lancelot is extremely attractive to women. Elaine, the Fair Maid of Astolat, dies of love for him; another Elaine, daughter of King Pelles, makes love to him (in the dark, he thinks she is Guinevere!) and their son Galahad does achieve the Grail; and he conducts a long, passionate, tempestuous affair with Queen Guinevere. At one point, after she jealously dismisses him, Lancelot lives in the wilderness and goes mad, but the queen's love is greater than her anger, and they resume their affair until King Arthur learns about it.

Lancelot and Guinevere's relationship leads to the disastrous break-up of the Round Table and collapse of Camelot. Knights take sides; old friends become new enemies; and Arthur has no choice but reluctantly to wage war against his dearest friend.

So for all his magnificence, Lancelot is a flawed and somewhat unbending figure, and he does not command quite the same sympathy as the king and queen. But his loyalty and love for Arthur never waver, and he comes with a huge army to help the king fight Mordred only to learn he is too late.

Guinevere, now a nun, tells Lancelot she will not see him again, and he becomes a hermit at Glastonbury. He dies soon after having a threefold vision of the queen's death, and his body is carried north and buried at Joyous Gard.

MORGAN LE FAY

Before giving birth to Arthur, Ygerna had a daughter by her first husband, Gorlois, Duke of Cornwall. This girl was called Morgan, and there were two sides to her character.

Good Morgan ruled the island away to the west known as Avalon. She was first in a sisterhood of nine healers and, when Arthur was grievously wounded, she took him to Avalon and promised to heal him. Fay means "fairy" and this good Morgan had magical powers: she could fly, she could change shape, and she was also a fine musician and poet. One romance refers to her as "Morgan the goddess" which suggests that, long before she appeared in Arthurian tales, she was thought to be a divine figure, maybe the Welsh Mother Goddess known as Modron.

Evil Morgan was a fascinating but destructive witch, and an enemy of Camelot. She fell in love with Merlin, and learned her magic from him. Envious of Arthur, she stole his scabbard (which protected him) and, after the king had put one of her many lovers to death, attempted to have him murdered. She hated Guinevere and tried to undermine the Round Table by using magic against one of its greatest knights, Sir Gawain.

Arms and Armour

The first thing you are likely to notice about a suit of armour is its weight. Armour is made of iron or steel and greatly slows down and restricts the movements of the man wearing it. A knight in armour wasn't even able to mount his own horse (spare a thought for the poor horse!) and had to be lifted on to it with poles and pulleys and ropes. And if he fell off, the knight lay on his back, like a beetle, unable to stand up unless someone helped him. His enemy was not always ready to help in this way!

Because armour is clothing, no suit of armour is quite like any other. It has to fit the shape and size of its owner, and it reflects changing fashions. Some rich knights had their armour made in Italy and Germany, just as today some people have their dresses made in Paris and their shoes in Milan.

People's feelings are affected by the clothes they wear. Knights in armour felt reasonably safe, certainly, but when they were wearing visors they also felt very confined and cut off:

> He (King Pellinore) got up facing the wrong way, and could not find Sir Grummore. There was some excuse for this, since he had only a slit to peep through – and that was three inches away from his eye owing to the padding of straw – but he looked muddled as well . . .
>
> "Take that!" cried Sir Grummore, giving the unfortunate monarch a two-handed swipe on the nob as he was slowly turning his head from side to side, peering in the opposite direction . . .
> "Where are you?" asked King Pellinore.

So says the twentieth-century novelist T. H. White!

Many romance writers delighted in describing how knights looked in their suits of armour as they rode on quests and into combat. But the helpful author of Sir Gawain and the Green Knight describes how a knight was actually armed, from the feet upwards – so that he wouldn't become top-heavy!

They fix steel sabatons (shoes) onto his feet,
Lap his legs in gleaming metal greaves (shinguards),
Their brilliant knee-joints newly burnished,
And fasten them, with knotted filigree, to his knees.
Fine thigh-pieces, lashed with leather thongs
Cover his thick thighs, and close over them.
A coat of link-mail, its rings glinting,
Clasps him round, over a vest of finest cloth,
Polished arm-pieces, with gay-coloured elbow-guards
Are fastened to his arms and, last, gauntlets of steel.

In the twelfth century, a knight's armour was much the same as it had been for generations of Saxon and Celtic warriors before him: no more than a helmet and a stiff leather jerkin or waistcoat – basic protection for head and body. But during the thirteenth and fourteenth centuries, armour for a man, and sometimes for his horse, became increasingly complex (and expensive) so as to protect the whole body against an increasingly dangerous range of weapons.

For the most part, Saxons, Celts and Vikings relied on cumbersome shields, spears and battle-axes – and their literature, jewellery and grave-goods point to how central weapons were to their way of life. The very word "Saxon" derives from *seax*, a kind of long penknife. Men in a medieval army continued to use spears and axes as well as much lighter shields, but they also carried long bows and crossbows made of yew wood, with a supply of arrows fledged with goose-feathers; they carried lances and daggers (which hung on a man's right side) and maces, which were nasty, metal-headed and sometimes spiked, clubs.

But throughout the Middle Ages the most prized weapon of all was the sword, its springy blade made of steel, sometimes engraved with patterns, and up to three feet long. Swords often outlived their owners and became valuable heirlooms, while the swords of some heroes had their own names: Naegling belonged to Beowulf, Flamberge to Charlemagne, Durendal belonged to Roland, Excalibur to Arthur.

Gunpowder was first imported into Europe from the east in the early fourteenth century. It has no part to play in the story of King Arthur and his knights; but by the time Sir Thomas Malory was writing *Le Morte d'Arthur* in the middle of the fifteenth century, it was already beginning to make heavy armour pointless and a thing of the past, and changing the whole way people waged war.

The Arming of Sir Topaz

They fetched him first the sweetest wine,
Then mead in mazers they combine
 With lots of royal spice,
And gingerbread, exceeding fine,
And liquorice and eglantyne
 And sugar, very nice.

They covered next his ivory flank
With cloth spun of the finest hank,
 With breeches and a shirt.
And over that (in case it fail)
A tunic, then a coat of mail,
 For fear he might be hurt.

And over that contrived to jerk
A hauberk (finest Jewish work
 And strong in every plate)
And over that his coat of arms,
White as a lily-flower's charms,
 In which he must debate.

His shield was of a golden red
Emblazoned with a porker's head,
 Carbuncles at the side;
And there he swore by ale and bread
That he would kill the giant dead,
 Betide what might betide!

Boiled leather on his shins had he,
His sword was sheathed in ivory,
 His helm was copper bright.
His saddle was of narwhal bone,
His bridle shone like precious stone,
 Or sun, or moon at night.

THE CANTERBURY TALES: GEOFFREY CHAUCER

mazers: drinking-cups
hauberk: a coat of chain mail
narwhal: an Arctic sea-beast with a spirally twisted straight horn

TOURNAMENTS AND TILTING

Tournaments were war games. They were a way in which young and middle-aged men could lawfully flex their muscles and display high spirits and love of risk while at the same time developing their military skills:

> The famous King Richard (Richard the Lion Heart), seeing the extra training and instruction of the French made them that much fiercer in battle, wanted the knights of his kingdom to train in England, so they could learn from tourneying the art and technique of fighting, and so that the French could not insult the English knights for being crude and less skilled.

So says the medieval historian, William of Newburgh.

During the twelfth century, tournaments often turned into brawls. Dozens or even hundreds of knights and squires met and divided into two teams. There was no playing field and there were few rules. Roaming all over the countryside and even through city streets, the players aimed to dismount their opponents and capture them and their horses. At some tournaments, defeated knights had to pay ransoms to buy back their freedom; at some, they didn't get their valuable warhorses back at all; and although a tournament was an exercise and a celebration, participants were sometimes wounded, and from time to time accidentally killed.

Because tournaments (sometimes known as Round Tables) were becoming increasingly popular, sizeable and unruly, King Edward the First made laws for them in 1274: no knight was allowed to bring more than three attendants, and players were to use only blunted swords.

So what had started (in northern France at the end of the eleventh century) as a sometimes joyous, sometimes furious scrum, was beginning to change into an organized game. And what had started as a team event was also becoming a sport for individuals. A tournament could include single combat within an enclosed field, known as jousting. Or it could feature tilting, when two knights rode straight at each other down two narrow lanes (or lists) divided by a rail (or tilt) to keep the horses apart. They carried blunted lances and their aim was to unseat each other.

These events were not only competitions but, as we read in Arthurian Romances, magnificent social occasions, attended by ladies and crowds of spectators. Knights and squires were the players, heralds acted as judges (*diseurs*), and ladies gave the winners splendid prizes: diamonds, rubies, gold chains, a helmet, a length of cloth and, on one occasion, a talking parrot;

Vermilion and blue and white: many a banner was flying there, and so was many a lady's wimple and sleeve, given as a love token. Many a lance was raised there, some painted in silver and red, some in gold and blue, some striped, some spotted . . . And there were so many splendid horses, some dark with white patches, others sorrel or tawny or white or black or bay. The knights all charge at each other at top speed. The whole field is covered with arms. Both sides shudder as they clash, and then there is an enormous din. Lances break, shields are holed, horses sweat or lather, riders tumble from their saddles.

EREC AND ENIDE: CHRÉTIEN DE TROYES

HERALDRY

King Arthur had a dragon banner and a dragon on top of his helmet. And each of the knights of the Round Table carried a colourful shield with his personal design on it. The use of these designs is known as heraldry. Sir Kay, head of the king's household, has two keys on his shield; Sir Gawain has a five-pointed star, and the points stand for his virtues; Sir Yvain has a lion because he fought a lion; and Sir Lancelot has three scarlet strips to indicate that he has the strength of three men. In this way, a shield design often symbolized its owner's outstanding characteristic.

The reason why knights decorated their shields, put crests on their helmets and wore decorated linen coats (this is where the word "coat-of-arms" comes from) over their armour is simple: it was a matter of recognition. Knights wearing armour and visored helmets look very much the same as one another and, in battle, a man needed to be able to single out his leader, and to be absolutely sure who were his friends and who were his enemies.

The devices and emblems and patterns known as coats-of-arms belonged to an individual, and were passed from father to son. That is to say, they were hereditary. And within one family, each son, brother and nephew carried slightly different coats-of-arms to distinguish them from each other.

Each area of knowledge and activity has its own fascinating terms: winger and goalie; casting and playing; stave and crochet. The same is true of heraldry: a coat-of-arms has its field and divisions. Label and crescent and molet and martlet and annulet are the devices which distinguish first, second, third, fourth and fifth sons; and the words for the seven tinctures come from medieval France – *or* (gold or yellow) and *argent* (silver or white), *gules* (red), *sable* (black), *vert* (green), *azure* (blue) and *purpure* (purple).

There was a time when heraldry was free for all. But by the end of the Middle Ages, a coat-of-arms was a mark of particular distinction and privilege, like knighthood itself. King Henry the Fifth's heralds were responsible for proclaiming tournaments, and he appointed one of them to a position which still exists today known as Garter King of Arms, and it was up to him to decide who could be a coat-of-arms and who could not. Writers of Arthurian Romance often refer to heraldry, and one of the greatest, Chrétien de Troyes, was himself a herald.

TRISTAN AND ISOLDE

The passionate and tragic love of Tristan and Isolde was one of the most popular love stories in medieval Europe.

Isolde, an Irish princess with the gift of healing, is betrothed to King Mark of Cornwall. But on her way to her wedding at Tintagel, she and Sir Tristan (who is King Mark's nephew) unwittingly drink a magic love potion, and at once fall wildly in love. Isolde goes ahead with her marriage, but she and Tristan, who is a dragon-slayer and a fine harpist, continue their love affair.

In his romance *Tristan* (early thirteenth century), Gottfried von Strassburg shows this love as something more glorious than terrible. The lovers are deceitful and desperate, and they break the rules of society and church; yet they are so utterly committed and so rapturous that they somehow create their own rules and can only be wondered at, pitied and forgiven:

Tristan, Isolde; Isolde, Tristan;

A man, a woman: a woman, a man.

King Mark learns the truth; Isolde is banished; the lovers live in a forest cave; then Isolde returns to her husband and Tristan goes into exile. But the unhappy king acknowledges the enduring force of their passion by having them buried together. A vine grows out of Tristan's grave and a rosebush out of Isolde's grave. They meet and entwine, once upon a time and forever.

Little Girls

A girl's hair is usually more wavy and softer than a boy's, and her neck is longer. The female complexion is generally fairer than the male, and the face more cheerful, gentle, calm and friendly. From the shoulders to the navel the body of a girl is narrower than a boy's, but from her navel to her knees it is wider. A girl's fingers and toes are more elegant and less stiff. Her voice is gentle; she is quick to speak and has plenty to say; her steps are shorter and more constricting than those of a boy. And her spirit: it is cheeky and easily annoyed, full of temper and forgiveness and jealousy and impatience, easily influenced, sly, and sharp, and determined to get its own way at once.

ON THE PROPERTIES OF THINGS: BARTHOLOMEW THE ENGLISHMAN

Love

Nowadays, men can't love women for seven nights before insisting on having their way. It stands to reason this kind of love won't last, for when people do something quickly and hastily, the heat soon cools. And that's how love is these days, soon hot, soon cold. There's nothing constant about this. But love in the old days wasn't like this. Men and women could love each other for seven years without lecherous desires coming between them, for at that time love entailed solemn promises and faithfulness. And this was the kind of love that was known, too, in the days of King Arthur.

LE MORTE D' ARTHUR: SIR THOMAS MALORY

93

MEDIEVAL ART

The world of King Arthur is still so widely recognized as a Golden Age that many companies, clubs and businesses in modern Europe and America use passwords connected with it – Round Tables of business, New Age Avalon stores, Excalibur razor-blades, Camelot candies.

In medieval Europe, Arthurian legends were used in a different way. As the romances became more and more popular, with scribes painstakingly copying them out over and over again, and illustrating their manuscripts with glowing, startlingly fresh colours, people liked to use characters, situations and scenes from them to decorate an astonishing array of artefacts.

Maybe there was an Arthurian lady waiting for you in your bedroom, adorning your bedcover or the back of a mirror, your ivory pin-box or wooden medicine-chest or bone comb. Or else there were Arthurian

knights and ladies downstairs in the hall, riding round a drinking-cup or peering up from a tray, or portrayed on the embroidery or tapestry hanging on the wall.

One very rich family owned a model ship (known as a nef) with three masts and a panoply of sails, all made of silvergilt; the ship itself, a nautilus shell, sits on the back of a mermaid; and on board are the lovers Tristan and Isolde, playing chess and holding hands.

Or maybe the king was waiting for you in church! You might stare at a stained glass window showing Arthur as a great Christian or British king. You might walk to your place across red clay tiles depicting a now-forgotten legend – King Arthur riding a goat and fighting a giant cat, King Arthur fighting a dragon. You might sit on a hinged seat with a wooden carving (called a misericord) under it, such as the one showing Sir Yvain's poor horse being cut in half by a falling portcullis.

These objects were all made between five and eight hundred years ago, and each speaks for the dozens and dozens broken and thrown away, eaten by mice, or just crumbled into dust. That so many artefacts do survive, among them the grander Round Table at Winchester or the magnificent murals by Pisanello (c. 1395-1455) at Mantua in Italy, tells us just how popular the world of Arthur was in the Middle Ages.

WILDERNESS

Mountains and moors, forests and fens, sandy heaths and saltwater marshes: wild places and the wildlife they support have come to matter deeply to many of us today. But medieval men and women viewed the wilderness as uncivilized and unattractive and dangerous, a place where the huntsman went of necessity but where other human beings were exposed to the elements, robbers, wild men of the woods, wild beasts, and all kinds of monsters.

So of course Arthurian Romance writers used the wilderness as a way of testing their heroes. To prove his manliness and chivalry, a questing knight had to turn away from the safe and shapely world of castle and town, herb-garden and knot-garden, and the grazing fields surrounding them, and ride out to face the wild:

> Among those hills he found so many marvels
> It's hard to tell a tenth part of them all.
> Sometimes he wars with dragons or with wolves,
> With horrible half-men who kept the woodland crags;
> With bulls and bears; sometimes with savage boars,
> And giants from the high fells, who followed him . . .
> But, if those fights were fierce, winter was worse,
> When chilling water spilled out of the clouds,
> Freezing as it fell, pelting the pale ground.

QUESTS AND ADVENTURES

Aquest is a long journey containing many difficult and maybe dangerous adventures, and it always has a purpose. This purpose or goal is sometimes a meeting, sometimes a rescue attempt, sometimes a treasure, sometimes a place. Medieval Sir Gawain, travelling north from Camelot to keep his promise to meet the magical and terrifying Green Knight whom he has already beheaded, and modern Mother Teresa on a mission to save defenceless people from suffering and evil, modern Richard Branson, trying to sail round the Earth in a hot-air balloon, and medieval Sir Galahad searching for the Holy Grail: all four are on a quest.

But in some Arthurian Romances, the point of the quest is the journey itself. In *Erec and Enide*, Chrétien de Troyes describes how the newly-married Sir Erec is taunted by his fellow knights with spending all day in bed, and sacrificing his knighthood for love; Sir Erec responds by angrily leaving court with his wife, and riding out to face a string of fearsome adventures, so as to prove the strength of her commitment to him and his commitment to chivalry.

Whatever his goal, a knight on a quest has to go to the limit and come face to face with himself. He must remain courteous, despite the greatest provocation; he must face natural and supernatural powers with equanimity; and he must be a highly-skilled man of war who proves himself by fighting worthwhile enemies. After all, no one becomes famous by killing sheep. Like the Anglo-Saxon poet who composed *Beowulf*, Arthurian Romancers knew that "Strong men must seek fame in far-off lands".

A number of quests begin in the same way. King Arthur and his knights are together at Camelot or Caerleon or Carlisle, but the king will not eat until he has heard or seen "a great marvel". Then a stranger arrives at court:

A young woman came into the hall and greeted the king and asked for help.

"Whose help?" asked the king. "What is the adventure?"

"Sir," said the young woman, "I am in service with a lady. She is well known and greatly respected – but a cruel knight is besieging her castle; she can't even escape from it. And because the knights here are known as the greatest knights in the world, I have come to beg for your help."

"What is your lady's name, and where is her castle, and who is the knight besieging her, and what is his name?"

"Sir," said the young woman, "I will not tell you my lady's name here and now, but I assure you she is greatly respected and owns many estates. As for the tyrant besieging her and wrecking her land, he is called the Red Knight of the Red Lands."

So this stranger at court, often a young woman, asks King Arthur for

help, knowing the king and his knights are pledged to protect the weak, and defend right against wrong. Now King Arthur hands down the challenge, and asks his knights which one of them is willing to undertake the quest. Sometimes there are plenty of takers, and sometimes an unexpected volunteer such as the kitchen boy called Beaumains (because of his large and beautiful hands); but sometimes no one wants to take up the challenge. "All right, then," says King Arthur on one occasion, "I'll have to do it myself." And his words at once shame his nephew, Sir Gawain, into offering to take the king's place.

The most challenging of all quests was for the chalice used by Christ and His disciples at the Last Supper, known as the Holy Grail. Whereas other quests tested a Christian knight's chivalry, the Grail quest tested and proved his behaviour as a Christian; and the two were not quite the same!

Only three knights succeeded. Sir Galahad promptly expired in joy! Sir Perceval stayed at the Grail Castle as the Grail's new guardian, known as the Fisher King. Sir Bors alone returned to Camelot after seeing the Grail, "and everyone at court was overjoyed to see him."

THE QUESTING BEAST

King Arthur was one of the very few people who ever caught sight of the Questing or Yelping Beast, and he thought it was "the strangest beast that ever he saw or heard of": it had a head like a snake, a leopard's body and a lion's backside, and feet like a hare. Many knights, however, did hear the creature baying in the distance, and said it sounded as though it had sixty hounds inside it.

King Pellinore spent years pursuing this elusive beast, vowing that "either I shall achieve him, or bleed of the best blood of my body", and after his death Sir Palamedes took up the chase.

One romancer wrote that the Questing Beast was actually the offspring of an evil princess and the Devil, but another claimed it was spotlessly white with emerald eyes and was terrified by its own noise. I think of this absurd animal neither as pure nor wicked but as a kind of send-up of the knightly quest: for what is the point and where is the honour in hunting and trying to kill a creature that harms nobody and is in any case almost impossible to find?

MAGIC AND THE OTHERWORLD

Arthur's life begins with Merlin's magic, and does not end because of Morgan's magic. In almost every romance, magic is a force in much the same way as it is in folk-tales about human encounters with fairies, giants and fabulous beasts.

This magic is of several kinds. People in the Middle Ages believed Heaven and Hell were real, physical places; and they half-believed in the Island of Avalon, away to the west, and the underground kingdom of Annwn, a magical otherworld inhabited by demons and their red-eared hounds.

But Arthurian knights and ladies didn't have to go as far as that to see magical beings. There were magicians and enchanters, sorcerers and necromancers all around them. The wizard Merlin uses his powers to protect Arthur until his beautiful apprentice Nimue turns his own magic against him; the Lady of the Lake gives Arthur Excalibur; and Morgan le Fay tries to destroy King Arthur's marriage by conjuring up a lookalike Guinevere.

Questing knights met not only terrifying shape-changers but supernatural beings, fabulous beasts and paranormal structures and objects. Sir Lanval makes love to a beautiful fairy woman; King Arthur fights against Ritho, the giant of Mount Snowdon who wears a cloak made of the beards of warriors whom he has killed; Culhwch chases the ferocious wild boar Twrch Trwyth from Ireland across to Wales, and from Wales down into Cornwall; Sir Lancelot crosses a bridge made of swords, Sir Perceval stops a castle spinning in the air, and Sir Yvain finds a spring that will cause a wild storm when water from it is poured over an emerald.

Much of the magic in Arthurian legend come from its early Welsh sources. This is partly because those sources are not romances but much older mythical tales in which humans are part of a larger universe, partly because of the quite extraordinary colour and wildness of the Celtic imagination. We should remember, too, that medieval men and women had a deeper communion with the natural world than we, and understood how each drop of water, leaf and stone has an energy of its own.

Tristan and Isolde drink a potion and immediately fall in love, the court at Camelot sees and cannot see the Holy Grail, and Sir Lancelot three times has a vision of the death of Queen Guinevere on the night before she dies. In such ways, the romance writers used magic to make magic, and created unforgettable illustrations of human joy, longing and sorrow.

The Magicians

Annowre She puts King Arthur under a spell but is unable to persuade him to become her lover. She is killed by Sir Lancelot.

Esclarmonde She is turned into a fairy. Her husband Huon succeeds Oberon as ruler of the kingdom of the fairies.

Lady of the Lake Several women are known by this name. One gives Arthur his sword Excalibur; one is apprentice to Merlin; and one is beheaded by Sir Balin.

Lunette (see under Leading Ladies)

Mabon He is stolen from his mother when he is only three days old, and taken to the Otherworld. He helps Culhwch win Olwen by running down the ferocious boar Twrch Trwth and seizing the razor and comb from between his ears.

Merlin He is the greatest of the magicians. He assists four successive kings of Britain, prepares Arthur for kingship, makes prophecies, and is imprisoned inside a rock by his own apprentice, Nimue.

Morgan le Fay She is a witch who tries to undermine the Round Table and destroy her half-brother King Arthur, but also a healer who rules the island of Avalon.

Nimue She is Merlin's beautiful young apprentice. When he becomes infatuated with her, she imprisons him inside a rock. She is also known as Viviane and Nineve.

Tyronoe She is Morgan le Fay's sister.

THE
HOLY GRAIL

At the Last Supper, Christ gave his disciples wine and told them it was the blood he was about to shed for them by sacrificing himself on the cross. The cup or chalice from which they drank is called the Holy Grail.

After his crucifixion, Christ's body was given for burial to Joseph of Arimethea. Joseph was a tin-trader, and he is said to have come to England, and to Glastonbury, soon after this to buy Cornish tin and Mendip lead, bringing with him the Holy Grail, the spear used by Longinus to pierce Christ's side on the cross, and a little bottle of Christ's blood. He hid them in the well beneath Chalice Hill, where the water is reddish-brown because it has iron in it.

One place at the Round Table is always left empty: the Perilous Seat, reserved for the knight who succeeds in finding the Holy Grail. After the Grail momentarily floats in front of King Arthur and his knights at Camelot, hidden in a dazzling shaft of sunlight, many knights set off in search of it, each knowing this will be his greatest test of all: the proof of whether he is not only brave, skilful and honourable but also truly Christian. For in the Holy Grail, man and God, and woman and God, meet and merge.

It is crucial that one knight should succeed. The guardian of the Grail, known as the Fisher King, has been badly wounded and is in agony; and he rules over a parched and sterile Waste Land. Only when a knight of the Round Table reaches the Grail can he be healed and allowed to die, and his Waste Land become green and fertile again.

Many romance writers were fascinated by the quest for the Holy Grail. They describe how Sir Gawain fails because of his lack of charity and faith; and how Sir Lancelot fails because of his adultery with Guinevere, permissible according to the rules of courtly love but sinful in Christian

terms. According to different romances, only the virgin knight Sir
Galahad (son of Sir Lancelot), innocent, child-like Sir Perceval and plain,
unpretentious Sir Bors actually achieve the quest for the Holy Grail:

> Then they looked and saw a man rise out of the holy vessel, and
> his wounds were those of Christ on the cross, and they were
> bleeding openly. And he said: "My knights, and my servants
> and my true children, who have come out of dead material
> into spiritual life, I will no longer hide myself from you."

The Corpus Christi Carol

Lulli, lullay, lulli, lullay;
The falcon has carried my mate away.

He carried him up, he carried him down,
He carried him into an orchard brown.

In that orchard there was a bed,
Hung with gold shining red.

And in that bed there lies a knight,
His wounds bleeding day and night.

Beside that bed a young woman stays,
And she sobs by night and day.

And beside that bed there stands a stone,
Corpus Christi engraved thereon.

ANONYMOUS

The Magical Objects

Excalibur The sword given by the Lady of the Lake to King Arthur. Its scabbard protects the king's life.

The Glass House This is invisible, and it is where Merlin may still live. It may be on the island of Bardsey and may be somewhere out to sea.

The Glastonbury Thorn A species of hawthorn which is said to have sprung from Joseph of Arimethea's staff, and which blossoms at midwinter.

The Holy Grail The chalice used by Christ and his disciples at the Last Supper. Many knights quest for it, but only three are so chivalrous and so Christian that they succeed.

The Round Table The enormous circular table at which each of King Arthur's knights had his own seat.

The Sword in the Stone This appears in a London churchyard, embedded in an anvil. By drawing it from the anvil, Arthur proves he is the rightful king of England.

The Wheel of Fortune A great wheel held by the goddess Fortuna. Nine heroes (three Biblical, three pagan and three Christian) cling to the rim, some on their way up, some on their way down.

SIR MORDRED

A horrible character, a horrible life and a horrible death: Sir Mordred is the greatest villain in Arthurian Romance, but he is also born a victim.

Mordred was conceived when King Arthur made love to his own half-sister Morgause, not realizing they were related. When he discovers the truth, Arthur tries to send Mordred to his death, but Mordred survives a shipwreck, and joins the Round Table. There, he soon wounds Arthur by telling him Guinevere and Sir Lancelot are lovers. The king still puts his son in charge of the kingdom when he leaves Camelot for France, to fight Lancelot; but embittered Mordred announces the king has been killed, usurps the throne and has himself crowned at Canterbury. He then tries to seduce his own horrified stepmother, Guinevere.

But Mordred's last deed is his worst. When his father comes home, he raises a huge army and fights against him at Camlann. Arthur spies Mordred, "that all this woe hath wrought," standing beside a heap of dead bodies, and runs straight at him, bawling "Traitor, now is thy death day come." So Arthur kills his own son, and Mordred savagely wounds his father by piercing his skull.

SIR BEDIVERE

One-handed Sir Bedivere is King Arthur's cupbearer and his most loyal companion. When the king is on his way to attack Rome with an army of 183,000 men, he crosses the path of the child-strangling giant of Mont St Michel in Brittany, and it is Sir Bedivere alone who helps him kill this monster.

Years later, King Arthur fights his last battle against his own son, Mordred, and it is Bedivere alone who survives it. Lying wounded on the battlefield, the king tells him to hurl his sword Excalibur into the water. Twice Bedivere disobeys. "Who would have thought I could have loved you or that people think you are noble," says Arthur, "when you're ready to betray me for a valuable sword?" Arthur is right to appeal to Bedivere's sense of loyalty and the knight goes down to the water for a third time and hurls Excalibur into it. Then he carries his dying king down to a barge full of beautiful women, and watches the barge sail away.

And as soon as Sir Bedivere had lost sight of the barge, he wept and wailed, and so took the forest; and so he went on all that night.

Last Rites

Then Sir Bedivere shouldered the king and carried him down to the water. A little barge with many beautiful ladies in it was waiting for them there; amongst them was a queen, and they all wore black hoods, and all wept and shrieked when they saw King Arthur.

"Now put me in the barge," said the king.

And Sir Bedivere did so, gently. Three queens received him from Bedivere, sobbing; they laid him down, and King Arthur pillowed his head in the lap of one of the queens.

And then that queen said: "Ah, dear brother! Why have you delayed so long? Alas, this wound on your head has grown too cold."

And so then the ladies rowed away from the bank, and Sir Bedivere watched as they left him.

Then Sir Bedivere cried, "Ah, my lord Arthur! What will become of me now you are going away, and leaving me here alone among my enemies?"

"You must comfort yourself," said the king, "and do as best you may, for you can no longer trust in me. I must go to the vale of Avalon to heal my deep wound: and if you never hear of me again, pray for my soul."

LE MORTE D'ARTHUR: SIR THOMAS MALORY

AVALON & GLASTONBURY

Avalon is an island somewhere to the west. Its name is Celtic and probably means "Isle of Apples", a fruit with magical properties, as we know from the Garden of Eden, the golden Apples of the Hesperides, and the apples of youth of the Norse goddess Idun. Another name for the island is "Fortunate", so Avalon and the earthly paradise of Celtic mythology known as the Fortunate Isles may be one and the same place.

Arthur's sword Excalibur was forged in Avalon, and he was taken there after the Battle of Camlann. The ruler of the island, Morgan le Fay, "laid the king . . . on a golden bed, unbandaged his wound with her fair hands, and stared at it. At last she said she could cure him if he would stay with her for a long time and agree to her treatment."

In 1191, monks at Glastonbury Abbey in Somerset (which means Summer Land) found a lead cross inscribed HIC IACET SEPULTUS INCLITUS REX ARTURIUS IN INSULA AVALONIA (Here lies buried renowned King Arthur in the island of Avalon). Nine feet below, the

monks found a hollowed-out log containing the bones of a man and a woman. Avalon, said the monks, was Glastonbury! But which came first? Did they fake the grave to back up an old tradition that Arthur had been buried at Glastonbury? Or did they call Glastonbury Avalon only after finding the grave?

The claim of the monks is not impossible. Misty Glastonbury, with its vast, ruined abbey (once the most powerful in England), was at one time almost an inland island, built around the Tor and Chalice Hill and surrounded by lakes and marshes. So your choice of Avalon may depend on whether you think Arthur died of his wounds or lies healed and sleeping, and will one day return.

But to visit Glastonbury – in your mind or on your feet – is in any case to draw near with Arthurian faith. The tradition connecting Joseph of Arimethea's staff with the Glastonbury Thorn, a Near Eastern species of hawthorn which blossoms in late December or early January, may only be a couple of hundred years old; but Glastonbury is where Joseph is said to have brought and left the chalice (or Holy Grail) used by Christ and his disciples at the Last Supper. It is where Guinevere was abducted; it is where Lancelot lived as a hermit, and where Sir Bedivere hurled Excalibur into the water. Centuries pass but its ancient ground still somehow embodies Arthurian mysteries.

ARTHUR'S BRITAIN

Britain, says one medieval poet, is a place

> Where war, and joy, and terror
> Have all at times held sway;
> Where both delight and horror
> Have had their fitful day.

Because of its long history, the British landscape is layered with memories: haunted house and deep ditch, battlesite and hidden pool all have historical or legendary tales to tell. So it is scarcely surprising that well over sixty places in Wales, Scotland and England are said to be connected with its greatest hero.

Although the "historical" King Arthur and his followers lived in the fifth or sixth century, Arthur has long been linked with man-made monuments much older and much more recent than that. Stonehenge, for instance, was erected during the Neolithic Age, about 4000 years ago. But Geoffrey of Monmouth writes that Uther Pendragon (Arthur's father) got 1500 men to work with hawsers and ropes and scaling ladders and "every conceivable kind of mechanism" to bring the stones from Ireland to Britain. When they failed, Merlin burst out laughing and raised the stones, and brought them to England by ship, thus proving that his artistry was worth more than any brute strength.

There are Roman defences, Iron Age hillforts, Norman castles and medieval cathedrals and churches with Arthurian connections. Arthur and Mordred are said to have fought their Battle of Camlann near Hadrian's Wall at Birdoswald. Bamburgh Castle and the castle at Alnwick are believed to be one and the same as Lancelot's Joyous Gard. And King

Arthur and his warriors come down from Cadbury Castle in Somerset each Christmas Eve to drink from the well near Sutton Montis church.

Other tales and traditions, some of them very old, associate Arthur with singular features of the natural landscape: hilltop and outcrop of rock, rocky pillar, river and lake. A cliff near Llangollen is called Craig Arthur (Arthur's Rock); the extinct volcano overlooking Edinburgh is known as Arthur's Seat. Some people say that Arthur never crossed the water to Avalon but is still alive, sleeping under Craig y Dinas, the "Rock of the Fortress" in the mountains north of Swansea, or somewhere inside the cliffs near Richmond Castle in Yorkshire.

There is much point in visiting these places. They are often striking in themselves. They excite our imagination and curiosity. And if we look and listen carefully, we may here and there catch something more – the echo of a memory.

Companies of Beasts and Birds

A muster of peacocks. An exaltation of larks.

A wakefulness of nightingales. A charm of goldfinches.

An unkindness of ravens. A clattering of choughs.

A pride of lions. A business of ferrets.

An impatience of wives. A doctrine of doctors.

A sentence of judges. A flattery of taverns.

A melody of harpers. A tabernacle of bakers.

A frenzy of maidens. A skulk of foxes.

A peep of chickens. An eloquence of lawyers.

A blast of hunters.

FROM THE BOKE OF ST ALBANS (1486)

THE KING WHO WAS AND WILL BE

Did King Arthur exist? Was there really a court called Camelot? Where exactly was Arthur's kingdom? When did he rule? And what was he like?

To begin with, we scarcely need to know. We read about the legends of Arthur, and are caught up in a long dream we hope will never end. But after a while we are bound to start asking hard questions: who and what, how and when, and where and why. To answer them means leaving behind the colourful images in this book – all the mock-wars and proving adventures and romantic love of medieval times – and becoming something of a detective.

For no, there never was a medieval Arthur, presiding over a court of strutting, quarrelsome knights and precious ladies. But yes, medieval men and women did believe that there had once been a historical King Arthur and Camelot. William Caxton says as much:

> Those that say or think there was never such a king called Arthur may well be thought foolish or blind, for . . . there is much evidence to the contrary . . . in a number of places in England there are still and always will be mementoes and memorials of him, and also of his knights.

But no again, medieval romance writers weren't much interested in the identity and lifestyle of this historical Arthur. They simply turned him into an imaginary medieval king.

There are two huge problems in hunting for the original King Arthur in the dark wilderness of early British history. The first is that, before the medieval period (1100-1500 AD), there are very few written sources to light the way. The second is that we have to travel through so many centuries. More than seven hundred years dawdled past after the Romans left Britain in 410 AD before Geoffrey of Monmouth thrilled medieval readers with his account of King Arthur, almost as long as the time between Geoffrey and ourselves.

But there are pointers, and one of them is the name Arthur itself. For a few generations after the Romans had gone, some parents in Britain went on calling their babies by Roman names, and that is what Arthur is – a Welsh version of the Roman name Artorius. In sixth-century Wales, the name Arthur suddenly became quite popular. Why? Were parents calling their sons after some popular hero, just as some children today are called after a well-known footballer or film star?

What written sources there are amount to little more than hints and scraps, and mostly come from a period later than this. There are

references to a leader called Arthur in eighth- and ninth-century Welsh manuscripts, known as the *Annals of Wales* and *The History of the Britons*, and the latter say Arthur was a leader of the Britons (the Celts) who fought and won twelve great battles against the Saxons: the twelfth battle was on Mount Badon, where 960 Saxons died during one day and one attack, and Arthur himself killed them all.

A sixth-century monk called Gildas also refers to this battle at Mount Badon – fought in about 500 AD, probably in the west of England – but alas! he doesn't even mention Arthur. Had he done so, our search for King Arthur would certainly be very much more easy.

What pointers there are do make clear Arthur was remembered as a warrior and a leader, living at a time when Britain was in a state of continuous and great ferment. The Romans had just pulled out; the British and Romano-British (people of mixed Celtic and Roman parentage) left behind were trying to organize themselves into a self-governing country; tribesmen (Angles, Saxons, Frisians, Jutes) from the Low Countries and Germany, long a thorn in the side of Roman Britain, were now trying to get a permanent foothold in England and pushing the Britons west.

This is the background to a scene in which some British leader organized and inspired his men (maybe in the north-west, more likely in the south-west), and stopped the Saxons in

their tracks by winning twelve victories in a row. This leader, a man living in a timber hall, side by side with his men and their animals within the stone walls of a windy Iron Age hill camp such as Cadbury Castle in Somerset: he is the nearest we can get to the historical Arthur.

The first complete poems and stories in which Arthur appears are Welsh. In one (dating from about 900 AD), King Arthur leads his followers on a raid to the otherworld on Annwn; and in another, the highly imaginative and entertaining *Culhwch and Olwen* (dating from the late tenth century), Arthur helps his young cousin Culhwch win beautiful Olwen as a bride by performing a string of amazing tests set by Olwen's father, who is a ferocious giant.

The Arthur of these tales is not at all the Arthur of later romances. He is the powerful and magical leader of a band of warriors in Cornwall, and the values of his court are the values of heroic society: readiness to lay your life on the line, physical bravery, a sense of humour and above all, fierce loyalty to your leader.

It is the twelfth-century Welsh priest Geoffrey of Monmouth who really stands at the gateway of medieval romance. He probably made use of sources now lost, but he was writing at a time when tribal feuding and Anglo-Saxon warfare had been replaced by the mock-enmity of tournaments and tilting, and when the crucial loyalty of lord and follower mattered less than the romantic love of man and woman. Geoffrey gave his readers a medieval king and court, but he was a Celt and he also celebrates the glory of the ancient Britons, and heaps fuel on the old British dream: that one day they will rise up, reclaim Britain and drive the Saxons back into the North Sea.

In this way, Geoffrey invented the ideal blueprint: a storyshape about a great hero with a wonderfully provocative outline but very little detail. Writers of romance loved it. Almost at once, they started to use and develop the story of Arthur, filling it with colour, energy, emotion and medieval ideals.

In the romances, we meet an Arthur who can be rather silly and wilful and doesn't mind offending his knights; an impatient Arthur; and a weary old Arthur who keeps tottering off to take a nap. But the romance writers also find much to agree about. Arthur is a great Christian king and a great British king. Even when Guinevere is unfaithful to him, he somehow never loses his stature or dignity; and most often he has a genuine nobility because he has a serious dream – to create a perfect society.

Some writer of Arthurian Romance understood, I think, our recurring belief, or at least longing to believe, that somewhere else, at some other time, there was harmony. This Golden Age is what is in Sir Thomas Malory's mind when Sir Gawain and many other knights vow to leave Camelot in search of the Holy Grail, and King Arthur sadly says:

Alas! Your vow is almost the death of me; for you have deprived me of the fairest and most honourable fellowship of knights who were ever seen together in any kingdom of the world . . .

So the legends of King Arthur and his knights and ladies at Camelot are, after all, a kind of dream. They are an ideal. This is why they fascinated medieval men and women and why they still matter so much to us. For there is a good part of each of us that longs for the better and the best. At this second millennium, our new Golden Age might include peace on earth, springing from our respect for each other, no matter what our gender, our colour, our culture, our class, our creed. It might include compassion and a sense of duty, and an end to hunger and disease. It might worship one God with many names. It might be coloured green.

We can dream this new, old dream because we are human and despite our human failings. It is what we really hope for when we say "The King Who Was and Will Be".

The First Book
Printed in English

I have worn out my pen writing this book, my hand aches and is none too steady, my eyes are dim from looking too long at the white paper, and I am not so inclined and eager to work as I used to be, my age creeps up on me day by day and weakens my whole body . . . Because of this, I have practised and learned at great care and cost to set this book in print in the manner and format you can see here. For it is not written with pen and ink, as other books are, and as a result everyone can have a copy at the same time.

THE RECUYELL OF THE HISTORIES OF TROYE: WILLIAM CAXTON

Index

Accolon, Sir   38
Agravain, Sir   38, 39, 63
Alexander the Great   71
Alfred the Great   41
Alnwick   43, 76, 114
Amesbury   73
Anguish, King of Ireland   62
Annowre   103
Annwn   101, 120
Arthur, King   18–19, 21, 23, 26, 29–31, 33–34, 36–43, 45, 50–51, 58, 60, 62–63, 69, 72–74, 76–78, 81, 88, 93–94, 97–101, 103–104, 107, 108–110, 112–115, 117, 119–121
Avalon   19, 78, 94, 101, 103, 112–113, 115, 118

Balin, Sir   33, 38, 103
Balmoral   45
Bamburgh   43, 76
Ban, King   76
Bardsey   27, 107
Bartholomew the Englishman   22, 92
Beaumains   63, 99
Bedivere, Sir   30, 33, 34, 109, 110, 113
Beowulf   81, 97
Bercilak, Sir   43, 68
Birdoswald   114
Bors, Sir   38, 99, 105
Boudicca   72
Breunor, Sir   38, 63
Brian des Isles, Sir   38
Brittany   63, 109
Broceliande   62, 63

Cadbury Castle   45, 115, 120
Cador of Cornwall, Sir   38
Caerleon   42, 45, 97
Cameliard   62
Camelot   38, 41-43, 45, 46, 47, 51, 62, 72, 73, 77, 78, 94, 97, 99, 102, 104, 108, 117, 121
Camlann   33, 34, 38, 108
Canterbury   108
Cappellanus, Andreas   56
Cardigan   42, 45
Carlisle   42, 45, 97
Carmarthen   26, 27, 42
   Castle   114
Caxton, William   17, 40, 74, 117, 122
Chalice Hill   104, 113
Charlemagne   18, 71, 81
Chaucer, Geoffrey   16, 82
Chester   42
Cold Ridge   31
Cole, King   72
Constantine, Sir   38
Corbenic   43
Cornwall   21, 31, 101, 120
Craig y Dinas   115

Culhwch   30, 63, 101, 103, 120
Cumbria   39

D'Orleans, Charles   55
David, King   71
de Troyes, Chrétien   17, 18, 56, 65, 69, 85, 89, 97
de Worde, Wynkyn   70
Dover Castle   40, 43
Dragonet, Sir   38

Ector, Sir   23, 26, 51
Edinburgh   115
Edward I, King   84
Elaine, the Fair Maid of Astolat   60, 62, 76
Enide   39, 62, 65
Erec, Sir   39, 62, 69, 97
Esclados   62
Esclarmonde   103
Ettard   62

Fisher King   39, 43, 99, 104
Fortuna   71, 107
France   46, 53, 58, 65, 72, 85, 88, 108

Gaheris, Sir   38, 39, 40, 63
Galahad, Sir   38, 76, 97, 99, 105
Ganieda   27
Garden of Eden   112
Gareth, Sir   38, 39, 40, 63
Gascony   65
Gawain, Sir   30, 38-40, 43, 62, 63, 68, 78, 79, 88, 97, 99, 104, 121
Geoffrey of Monmouth   19, 21, 27, 30, 114, 118, 120
Germany   53, 65, 119
Gildas   30, 119
Glastonbury   40, 73, 77, 104, 112, 113
Godfrey, Duke of Bouillon   24, 71
Gorlois, Duke of Cornwall   21, 26, 43, 63, 78
Gorre   76
Grail Castle   99
Green Knight   80, 97
Grummore, Sir   79
Guinevere, Queen   26, 36-40, 43, 56, 62, 65, 72, 73, 76-78, 101, 102, 104, 108, 113, 121

Hadrian's Wall   114
Hautdesert   43
Hector   71
Henry V, King   89
Henry VII, King   41
Henry VIII, King   36, 41
Huon   103

Idun   112
Ireland   26, 101
Isolde (see under Tristian)
Italy   95

Jerusalem   24, 46
Joseph of Arimethea   39, 104, 107, 113
Joshua   71
Joyous Gard   43, 76, 77, 114
Judas Maccabaeus   71
Julius Caesar   71

Kay, Sir   23, 30, 38, 39, 51, 88
King of Nantes   69

Lady of the Lake   26, 33, 34, 38, 76, 101, 103, 107
Lamorak, Sir   39, 63
Lancelot, Sir   38-40, 43, 56, 60, 62, 72, 73, 75-77, 88, 101-105, 108, 113, 114
Lanval, Sir   39, 58, 101
Laudine of Landuc   39, 62, 63
Layamon   36
Lear, King   72
Leland, John   45
Leodegrance of Cameliard, King   36, 37, 62
Lionors   62
Llangollen   115
Loholt, Sir   39, 51, 62
London   23, 26, 37, 45
Lot, King of Orkney   38, 40, 63
Lunette   63, 103
Lynette   39, 63
Lyonesse   63

Mabon   103
Maledisant   38, 63
Malory, Sir Thomas   17, 18, 23, 36, 37, 41, 60, 73-76, 81, 93, 110, 121
Marie de France   58
Mark, King of Cornwall   62, 90
Marlborough   27
Merlin   19, 21, 26-29, 33, 34, 36, 37, 42, 78, 101, 103, 107, 114
Modron   78
Mont St Michel   109
Mordred, Sir   38, 63, 72, 77. 108, 109, 114
Morgan le Fay   34, 38, 39, 63, 78, 101, 103, 112
Morgause   38, 40, 63, 108
Moronoe   63
Mount Badon   119
Mount Snowdon   101

Nimue (also known as Viviane and Nineve)   26, 33, 62, 63, 101, 103
Northumberland   38

Oberon   103
Odo, Cardinal   24
Olwen   30, 63, 103, 120
Owain, Sir   62, 63
Owen, Sir   39

Palamedes, Sir   39, 100
Paston, Agnes   68
Pelleas, Sir   62
Pelles, King   76
Pellinore, King   79, 100
Perceval, Sir   38, 39, 99, 101, 105
Philip of France, King   24
Pisanello   95
Provence   52

Red Knight   39, 63, 98
Red Lands   39, 63, 98
Richard, King (Richard the Lion Heart)   24, 84
Richmond Castle   115
Ritho   101
Roland   18, 81
Rome   71, 109
Romeo and Juliet   72
Russell, John   44, 64

Saladin   24
Sandringham   45
Scotland   114
Shakespeare, William   19
Somerset   45, 115
Stonehenge   26, 114
Sugyn   30
Sutton Montis   115
Swansea   115

Taliesin   30
Tintagel   21, 43, 90
Topaz, Sir   82
Tristian and Isolde   39, 56, 58, 62, 72, 90, 95, 102
Tyronoe   103

Urban, Pope   24
Uther Pendragon   21, 26, 37, 63, 114

von Strassburg   18, 90
Vortigern, King   26

Wace   36
Wales   26, 101, 114, 118
Waste Land   104
Westminster   40, 60, 62
White, T.H.   79
William of Newburgh   84
Winchester   36, 40, 41, 43, 45, 95
Windsor   45

Ygerna   21, 26, 63, 78
Ysbaddaden   30,63
Yvain, Sir   88, 95, 101